Bathinda to

Bathinda to Bangkok

Vibha Batra

BLOOMSBURY
NEW DELHI • LONDON • OXFORD • NEW YORK • SYDNEY

BLOOMSBURY INDIA
Bloomsbury Publishing India Pvt. Ltd
Second Floor, LSC Building No. 4, DDA Complex, Pocket C - 6 & 7
Vasant Kunj, New Delhi 110070

BLOOMSBURY, BLOOMSBURY INDIA and the Diana logo are trademarks of
Bloomsbury Publishing Plc

First published in India 2019
This edition published 2019

ISBN: PB: 978-93-88038-92-8; eBook: 978-93-88038-94-2

Typeset in Palatino by Manipal Digital Systems
Printed and bound in India by Thomson Press India Ltd.

To find out more about our authors and books visit www.bloomsbury.com and
sign up for our newsletters

For
BNPMSR

Acknowledgments

Thank you, *ji*, for joining thee B2B party and making it rocking-shocking. Now for some movies as return home gifts.

My family: *Carry on, Jatta*

My editor, Nandita: *Jihne Mera Dil Luteya*

My cover designer, Pallavi, from Graficus: *Vadhayiyaan Ji Vadhayiyaan*

My publishers: *Chak De Phatte*

My friends: *Yaaran Da Katchup*

My readers: *Young Malang*

To HP: *Control, Bhaji, Control*

1

The one with the (re) intro-shintro

BEEP! BEEP!

Uff! My cell *toh* should go inside Limca Book I thought, peesoing my teeth. Beeping thousand and one times in bloody one second.

BEEP! BEEP!

I took out breath and opened one eye – *chingggg* – like angry rishi (not Kapoor, saint). Checked out thee cell screen.

It was that Dingy. Dying again.

Actually, *she* should go inside Limca Book. For dying thousand and one times in bloody one day.

She was my bestie before testy (not exams, balls), but she was also little *jhalli*. Oho, why to lie, she was very *jhalli*. Sometimes *toh* I think my brain had gone to eat grass to start party-planning business with her. We were both 50-50 partners, but she couldn't do one thing 100% by herself. No, *ji*, not.

My yoga teacher had asked me to watch my breath during meditation. I watched as it came out of my ears.

BEEP! BEEEEP!

1

Ma ki@#$%!

I'd no choice only. I had to – *had to* – convert meditation to *pranayam*. I took deep breath, closed right nose with right thumb and covered left nose with three fingers. Then I picked up cell with left hand and stuffed it between right ear and shoulder.

'Hello?' I barked.

'M-m-m-Mahi?'

'No, Queen Victoria!' I replied, trying to hold on to cell and temper both.

'S-s-sorry Mahi, I know it's your off day. I know you said, "Dare you call between 12 and 1". I know you hate if someone does mother-sister of your meditation, but I'm f-f-finished –'

Hain?

She was f-f-finished? So soon? *Toh* she'd called me only to copy Shahrukh Khan?

'My life,' she sob-sobbed, 'it's over, finished, thee end.'

Oh!

'WAAAAAAA!'

Hai, she was crying like anything. In one second my heart melted like *kulfi* in heat. I removed thumb from right nose and took out breath. 'Oh, calm down, Dingy…just tell WWW…' (Oho, What Why When.)

'It's Andeep –'

'What did that *lallu* do now?'

'MAHIIIIII!' Dingy shouted. 'I told you not to talk like that! He's my *Fiancé*! Show some respect!'

I *was* showing respect. Inside-inside, I'd called him *laudu*.

'Okay, baba,' I said in soothing tone mother uses for baby. 'What did that Andeep do now?'

'He said, "Enough! Full stop! I can't convince Mummyji Daddyji anymore…there's no hope…they are not going to give blessings…I'm very sorry." Can you believe, Mahi?'

I could believe. That's why inside-inside I always called Andeep *laudu*.

'I also didn't keep quiet, told him straight on face, "Okay, then let's break up" because –'

'Because your dream's to get married in Bangkok,' I finished.

Most people wanted to go to Bangkok hiding-hiding for bang-bang. But Dingy was *Sanskari Bharatiya Nari, ji*. (Oho, Traditional Indian Woman.) She wanted to go there for humpy-pumpy with permission-slip from elders. She became tears-tears.

'If I can't get married in Bangkok,' she ate swear, 'if I can't get married in Bangkok –'

'You won't get married to him?' I asked, with hope in my voice.

Too much hope, because Dingy shouted, 'MAHI!' and started Round Two of crying. For thee next few seconds, she got busy blowing nose. Giving me time to finish one set of deep breathing. I was going to do one more, when she burst out, 'Help, Mahi-ve! Do something!'

'What can I do, *yaar*?'

'I don't know anything… I just know if anybody can do anything, it's you and only you…'

Oho, I was PC (not Priyanka Chopra, Sorcar) or what? As if I could do abracadabra on Andeep's parents and bring them under my control.

'Dingy, please, please understand. I also have some limits –'

'How can you ditch me and Andeep like this?' she cried, sounding like one-mad. 'Last year when you wanted help, who came in front? Andeep! Only Andeep! He helped you save Lavith –'

That's it. One small mention of *that* name was enough. I felt as if Dingy had taken rust-knife, heated it on stove, rubbed one kilo salt on it, and opened fresh wound in my heart.

'Yes or no, Mahi?

Yes.

'True or false, Mahi?'

True.

'Right or wrong, Mahi?'

Right.

Uff! Why was Dingy asking stupid-type questions? We were playing KBC – *Kaun Banega Chutiya* – or what? She knew what had happened. Leave her, full Ludhiana knew my history, geography, biology. My heart had been cut into *chintu* (not Rishi Kapoor, small) pieces in Delhi. And I was back to pavilion trying to join them like big puzzle.

'Andeep did you favour, Mahi, *big* favour. Now it's your turn.'

Oh, I *toh* felt like thee horse in Sholay. It was *izzat ka sawal*. Question of self-respect.

I let out long breath. What-what we had to do for friends. 'Dingy, I've to go –'

'Go? GO? *Hai Rabba!* I cannot believe,' Dingy screamed. 'After such emotional speech also, you're talking about going –'

'I've to go and make Bathinda plan, baba,' I said in Art-of-Leaving voice. 'That's where your in-laws live, *na*?'

For one second, Dingy lost her tongue. Then she shouted, tearing her throat, 'OYE MAHIIIIIII-*VE!*' She *toh* couldn't control only. All her feelings came out bubbling-bubbling. 'Thank you, thank you, thank you! I love you! You're piece of my heart, my life, my first love.'

Hai, she was touching me so much.

'Oho, stop maaroing senti,' I said, before I also got emotional. 'Bye now, I've to call my competition, Mr. Secondary.'

My meditation was fully working. Because in thee silence, I could hear Mahi smile.

'And one more thing –'

'*Uff!* Now what?' I asked impatiently. 'I made you sit on my shoulder, now don't do *susu* in my ear, okay?'

'Give me sorry, Mahi,' she said, doing sniff-sniff. 'Lakh-lakh times sorry. I shouldn't have mentioned last year and Lavi –'

'I-it-it's okay,' I quickly stopped her. I didn't want to hear that 'L' word again. 'Happens, *yaar.*'

'Okay, but I didn't mean to hurt you. God promise.'

'I know, Dingy, I know.'

She could never ever hurt me. At least, not like He (not god, that 'L' boy) had hurt me.

I cut thee call, my heart heavy like I'd eaten too many masala kulchas.

But I didn't call Andeep. I called Dumpy, Dingy's *bhraa* (not undergarment, big bro).

'Hello, hello, Mahi Madam!' he shouted into the phone. 'Long time, no news?'

'Sorry, Dumpy, I was too busy…'

My shoe, I was busy.

'Too busy for best friend?' he asked.

Hai, I *toh* didn't know what to say.

Actually, last year, full confusion had happened. Mistakes, misunderstandings, madness, what not. I'd made mistake of proposing to Dumpy, causing misunderstandings, leading to madness...don't ask. After that, on top-top, we maintained good relations, but inside-inside, things were stiff as starch shirt.

'Busy for gossip? He continued in leg-pulling voice.

Gossip? *Hai*, I *toh* need it like sari blouse needs booby pads.

'I thought when you heard about Ronit, you'd jump on phone and call me...'

He was telling truth. Thee whole world goes to Google-Shoogle or news channel for breaking news, I *toh* dial Dumpy.

'What to do, *yaar*,' I said slowly, trying not to sound despo to find out. 'Work's too much –'

'*Oye hoye*,' Dumpy said in teasing voice, 'I forgot that I was talking to best party-planner in whole of Ludhiana.'

'Only in Ludhiana?' I asked, making face.

I don't want to beat my own drum, but Ludhiana to London was not some *chunnu-munnu* local company. It also had some standard. With events in Goa, Delhi, Mumbai, it was full-on national. And with Dingy's Bangkok-Bang-Bang plan, it was going to reach international height.

'Okay, okay, your company's world-famous in India. Happy?'

'Hmm. Now you're coming on thee line,' I said in I-forgive-you voice. 'Okay, now what was that thing you were talking about?'

'What thing?' Dumpy asked. He was trying to act innocent but I knew his *rug-rug* (not carpets, veins).

'Something about that Ronit...'

'Oh, forget about that *chodu*...' Dumpy said.

Forget? After smelling blood, shark forgets, or what?

'Okay, fine! Bye, Dumpy, I'll call you later –'

'Mahi-ve,' he said in 'I'm-sorry' voice. 'I was just pulling your leg.'

'You've pulled leg, knee, thigh. Now tell WWW.'

'Okay, okay, can you believe his mother-in-law was having affair?'

I *toh* couldn't believe! 'Malhotra Aunty?'

'Ya! Malhotra Uncle caught her with red hands.'

'*Sauteli maa ki* @#$#!'

'Uncle was already having doubt. Day-night she was stuck to her cell. Not leaving it only, not for one second also. From kitty-party to *susu-potty*, she was taking it everywhere...'

'Then?' I asked, my ears singing.

'Then one day he heard her asking family tailor to put pockets in all her kurtas...'

Hain?

'....So she could put her cell phone inside, not miss any of her lover's calls,' Dumpy went on.

Oh!

'But who was her lover?' I just wanted him to come to thee point.

'Their family tailor, Daulat Ram!' Dumpy dropped atom bomb. 'He's really their "family" tailor now. Ha ha ha!'

Haw! What days had come! You *toh* couldn't trust your tailor also. One minute, he was taking your *naap* (not sleep, measurement), next minute, he was becoming your *bache ka baap*.

'But Malhotra Aunty was always going to temples –'

'Morning she was doing Ram-Ram, night she was doing Daulat Ram,' Dumpy said with chuckle. 'Anyways, leave. You didn't call me to hear about Aunty Affairs.'

'Actually, I wanted to talk to you about Andeep,' I confessed to him.

'Why, what did that *laudu* do now?'

Ya, everyone knew about Andeep. Except that blind-in-love Dingy.

'You know, *na*, Dingy wants to have first night in Bangkok – ?'

'What?'

'She wants destination wedding in Bangkok. But Andeep's parents want it in Bathinda.'

'Mad she is. Getting chance to dump him and not taking it.'

He was cent-percent correct. But what to do, I couldn't forget Dingy's CD (not compact disc, Crying-Dying).

'Crying-crying she's raised full sky on her head,' I informed him. 'Uncleji-Auntyji's don't have sense. *Arre*, they have no role to play in this film –'

'No, they are only thee boy's side,' Dumpy said in sarcastic voice.

I continued as if I hadn't heard. '...they are not hero-heroine, they are only side-actors. Andeep and Dingy get married in Thailand or Timbuctoo, what goes for them? They should quietly put tongue inside mouth and do *balle balle* in thee background...'

'But what role do you've to play in this?' Dumpy asked, confused.

'I have to, have to go to Bathinda. To put sense into their heads –'

SMACKKKKK!

Dumpy slapped his head loudly. 'Oh, so you want me to come to Bathinda with you. As your *driver* – ?'

Hai, Dumpy knew my *rug-rug*, too. But, my shoe, only I'd admit it.

'As Dingy's *Big B*,' I told him, my voice spicier than red chillies. 'You also have some responsibility or no? If you want to come, come. Or you also zip lips and sit quiet as mouse. As for driver, I can get ten like this,' I added, my fingers going click-click.

'Oh, Mahi-ve,' he said in 'Let's-make-up' voice. 'Your temperature's always on boiling point. Hundred-percent we'll come with you.'

'We?'

'Simran and me.'

SMACKKKK!

It was my turn to hit my head.

Simran. His girlfriend. She was ten times bigger *laudu* than Andeep.

'How long she's been asking me to take her for long drive,' Dumpy said, doing cluck-cluck. 'Poor thing.'

If Simran was poor thing, so was Mogambo.

'Four of us will go to Bathinda…'

Four? With common-sense, he'd lost counting power also.

'You, me, she. Three,' I said patiently.

'You forgot about Raj….'

Raj. Simran's twin brother. He was hundred times bigger *laudu* than Andeep.

'Her parents don't let her go anywhere without him.'

It was Buy One, Get One Free offer or what?

'You, me, she, he. Four.'

I hit my head four times.

Oho, I was jolly-type girl. I got along with all thee types of people – okay-okay, with some types of people. But thee day god had distributed brains in heaven school, Simran and Raj were absent, *ji*.

Hai, I thought in full panic, where I'd got stuck? I wanted to scream, shout, beat my chest like King (not raja, Kong). I wanted to throw my cell phone on wall. I wanted to cut cancel delete my own plan.

But when there's no choice, we've to listen to inside voice. It was question of Dingy's heart.

Mine was pieces-pieces, but I had to – *had to* – keep hers intact.

2

In which the heroine rushes to rescue a damsel (and dude) in distress riding on her (high) horse

'Okay, Dumpy,' I said, letting out long sigh. 'See you outside my house tomorrow morning –'

'Tomorrow?'

'Why, you've got appointment with Amitabh Bachchan?'

'No, but my store –'

Oh, I forgot to tell that he was thee owner of Dumpy Da Swag – Ludhiana's Number One Store for Number Two (not potty, fakes) things.

'Ask Dingy to sit there. You're doing this for her. She can do that much for you.'

Dumpy liked thee idea. After all, whose idea it was?

'Okay, see you at seven –'

'Seven?'

'If that's too late, we can leave at six,' I suggested sweetly.

'Nine, okay?'

He was bargaining like shopkeeper.

'Neither yours, nor mine,' I bargained like customer. 'Eight. Final deal or I'll ask someone else.'

'Done *dana-dan-dan!*' We reached settlement. 'Why don't you ask Niku also to join?'

Niku. My brother from another mother. But more own than my blood brother.

I lived with him and his mother. I called her Bhooto (short form for Bhootni). Why? Because she was such a sample, such a sample, don't ask.

As if she'd heard my thoughts, she suddenly yelled, 'MAHIIIIII!'

I got up and folded my yoga mat doing grumble-grumble. Not one second of peace in thee house. Now which mountain had fallen on Bhooto's head?

'MAH*IIII*! HELP! I'M *DYING*!'

Hai! I just threw thee mat to one side and went flying to her room. Thought I'd find her on floor, holding chest, life button going off.

No, *ji*, not.

She was full of life, spinning full speed on Aerobike, Everests (not mountains, boobies) shaking. She was dressed in her exercise clothes. Cotton salwar-kameez and keds, with dupatta tied like Miss Universe ribbon, dividing her XL body 50-50.

Uff! It was thee limit only.

'Mummyji!' I erupted like angry volcano. 'You said you were dying!'

'I am, *puttar*, I am…my throat – so, so dry.' She sounded like steam engine. Huff puff. Huff puff. 'Pass… pass…pass…' She pointed to Coke bottle on thee side table.

'Mummyji! Do you know how worried I was? I nearly got heart attack!'

'Me too,' she replied without stopping. 'All this exercise-vexercise…gasp, gasp…not…for… me.'

Whole world knew that. Thee last time fitness ghost had sat on her head, she'd bought very costly treadmill. Ya, she'd used it every day…to dry her bloody towel.

'Then why are you doing it?'

'My cholesterol level…it keeps going up and up –'

Arre, it was cholesterol, not her weight.

'Met Mrs Deol, she said better start HIWO,' she went puff and pant.

Hain?

'Highly Intense Work Out,' she explained.

Oh!

'When did you meet Mrs Deol?'

'Morning, at Hyatt Hotel.

'You went to Hyatt Hotel in thee morning?'

'Ya, for my Breakfast Kitty.'

My eyebrows flew to my forehead. 'You joined Breakfast Kitty!'

'Last month,' she informed me, wiping sweat rivers from her face. 'You're so busy, I forgot to tell.'

I was busy, so she forgot? *Macho,* Bhooto's logic could confuse Einstein.

I gave her my stern teacher look. 'So this is your…?'

She gave me blank look, winning Filmfare, Zee Cine, Sansui, TOIFA, IIFA – all Best-Actress Awards of thee year. 'This is my…?'

'Fifth? Sixth? Tenth kitty?' I burst out like water pipe.

'Touchwood!' she cried out, leaning dangerously – like racer on motorbike – to touch thee side of wooden side table. 'Mahi! I told you, roti or kitty – you should never count. Gets bad eye…'

I gave her bad look from my eye.

'Ah, aah, aaah,' she groaned, pressing her back. 'My slip disc…'

'You don't have slip disc.'

'Remember at that Khanna farmhouse, I slipped so badly…'

'*You* slipped and fell down, Mummyji, your disc was up only.'

'Ah, aah, aaah, my knees,' she groaned, pressing them, 'they are killing me.'

'Sure it's not thee breakfast you ate?' My voice was like Tabasco sauce.

'Where I ate? Just tasted little-little like bird…'

Little? Thee word itself was not there in PED – Pammi English Dictionary.

'Only cornflakes with milk – in *piddu* bowl.'

'So, you didn't have idlis?'

'Two idlis, *bas.*'

'Without coconut chutney?' I asked, fully knowing she ate chutneys like people eat daal. Bowl-bowl full.

'You want idlis to get stuck or what?' she replied, rubbing her neck.

'No dosa?'

'Four dosas –'

'Four!'

'They were mini dosas. This small.' Bhooto made O with her thumb and first finger.

'And your favourite – puri aloo?' I asked in challenging tone.

'Just two-and-half puris.'

'Why? What happened?'

'Wanted to keep place in my stomach for besan chillas,' she explained.

'So no place for pakoras?'

'Pakoras are like King's ride. Place is automatically made for them.'

I knew thee answer would upset me, but I couldn't stop. 'How many varieties?'

'Onion, paneer, cauliflower, chilli only.'

'Only,' I repeated, my voice like chilli.

'And corn cutlets.'

Uff! The whole menu was finished, but Bhooto was not.

'*Toh* you didn't have drinks?'

'Had, *na*. Orange juice, little sweet lassi, apple milk shake, banana milk shake…' She went on and on like she was Udipi hotel waiter. 'Everything was served in *ittu sa* glasses.' She made face as if the hotel had cheated her.

She wanted them to be served in jugs or what?

'If it's buffet, *paisa-vasool* izze must,' she announced her policy.

Typical mentality. All thee ladies of thee kitty had it. Eat double of what you spend. If everyone did *vasooli* like Ludhiana Loveleez (name of their WhatsApp group), all thee hotels would go bankrupt.

'But their sweet-dish counter was so-so,' she continued.

'So…?'

'So, ras malai, gulab jamun, moong dal halwa…'

Rabba! Her appetite was like Airtel's 4G offer. Unlimited.

'…and some Bengali sweet…that yellow one with malai on top…what's thee name…Dum Dum?'

'Cham Cham,' I supplied right answer.

'Ya.'

'Only Indian sweets, no Western?'

'Indo-Western,' Bhooto did chuckle-chuckle. 'Chocolate pastry was good, but strawberry mouse…'

'Mousse, Mummyji, mousse.'

'Ya, most ordinary it was…and those round rounds with jam inside – what do you call it…?'

'Swiss-rolls?'

'That's it.'

'That's it, that's all you ate? Or that's it, you were talking about Swiss-rolls?'

'That's it, I was talking about Swiss-rolls,' she took Option 1.

'You should have left something for the other guests also,' I said jokily outside.

Inside-inside, I needed Digene bottle, Pudin Hara tablets and Hajmola golis.

'Hope Sukhna comes back from thee market soon.…'

Sukhna. Our cook-cum-cleaner-cum lifeline. Without her, Ahluwalia household would have collapsed long back like that flyover in Kolkata.

'Have asked her to get chicken-rolls for lunch.'

Entire population of one small country could not *thooso* as much as she had. But Madam *Thoosam* was already talking about lunch.

'Chicken-rolls for lunch? Yummy,' Niku said, coming into thee room same way he'd come into my life. Like breath of fresh air.

My Daddyji (he became dear to God few years back) had married Bhooto when Niku and me were knee's height. From then till now, he was my favourite person in thee whole world.

'Niku!' I said happily.

'Mahi!' He smiled, showing all thirty-two.

Hai, it was so good to see his 1000 watt smile.

Same time, last year, his smile bulb had fused. Oh, it's very long story, Ashutosh Gowarikar film long. In short cut, *ji* – our family business was *thappp*. Niku needed money to start dream business but. Due to some legal problem, we couldn't sell our house, so he took illegal short cut. *Bas*, that's when thee *tatti* hit thee ceiling fan. And his smile went *phusss*.

Thanks to god, he had happy ending – means, his story had happy ending. We sold our big old house. Moved to small new one. In less posh area. Ya ya, Bhooto lost many BBFs (Bank Balance Friends). But Niku could finally start his dream business. He could open his ASS – Ahluwalia Super Store. From then till now, he was making blood and sweat one to make his ASS hit.

'Aah, my old bones cannot take it anymore,' Bhooto complained, braking suddenly, breaking my thoughts.

'But your cholesterol?' I asked with fake concern.

TING TONG!

'That must be Sukhna.' Forgetting about old bones, Bhooto jumped off thee aerobike with speed of young cheetah. 'Come, come, let's do stomach worship.'

We followed her to thee dining room like good little childrens.

Sukhna gave thee bill and Bhooto's BP went as high as her cholesterol. 'Six hundred rupees bill for chicken-rolls?'

'Breakfast buffet was how much?' I asked with sweet smile.

'Sixteen hundred after tax.'

Toh she could blow that much on herself, but not this much to feed her hungry naked childrens?

She took out roll of notes from her mobile wallet – oho, her bra – and gave them to Sukhna. 'God only knows where all my money is going…'

Inside your stomach, I wanted to say.

'Don't worry, Mummyji, I'm sure you're saving –' Niku began.

Saving? Thee word was Gujarati and Bengali to Bhooto.

'Where I'm able to save…after household expense, electricity, newspaper, maintenance, food, staff salary, I don't have one single pie left…oh, that reminds me, apple pie in thee buffet was not bad…'

I banged my head on thee dining table.

'Mahi!' Niku gave me concerned look. 'Are you okay?'

'Fine, fine. I just forgot to tell you, I'm going to Bathinda tomorrow –'

'Bathinda's butter chicken, yumm,' Bhooto licked her fingers, as if she could taste it long distance.

'Bathinda? With Dingy? To meet Andeep? To set wedding date? You said wedding's next year?' Niku hit me with questions like he was *Times Now* news wallah.

I sighed and told him everything A to Z. 'Want to join?' I asked after I finished.

'Can't.' Bhooto answered. 'My Kirtan Kitty is tomorrow.'

'Oh,' I said in fake sad tone. 'I'll miss you, Mummyji.'

'But if you want me to miss it – ?' she started.

'No, no,' I said quickly. 'Kitty and opportunity don't come every day.'

I turned to look at Niku.

'Sorry, *yaar*, can't –'

'Go, Niku, go,' Bhooto encouraged him. 'Don't work so hard. Last holiday you took was Goa…'

She stopped, guilty expression on her face. Oho, last year's *syaapa*? Only 50% had happened in Delhi. Other 50% took place in Goa.

I'd come back from Rape Capital one-and-half months back. From then, it was understood. That words connected to my past were banned. And thee ban was stricter than beef ban.

Bhooto looked at me with so much pity, so much pity as if I'd AIDS, cancer *and* sugar.

Niku smartly changed thee topic. 'So, what time tomorrow morning?'

'Eight.'

'Will give wake-up call at seven?'

I nodded fully gratefully. He was small brother with big heart.

KNOCK!KNOCK!

Sharp seven o'clock, my alarm clock gave wake-up call on my room door.

'Thank you, Niku. I'm awake,' I called out in *faku* sleepy voice.

Faku because I hadn't slept even *this* much.

It was like Mata Ka Jagran night for me. Whole-whole night I hadn't slept. But instead of being devotional for goddess, I was emotional over ex love God. Thee ban had been broken with LG (not electronics, Lavith-Goa) words. I'd tossed and turned, turned and tossed, thinking about thee past. Rewinding, fast forwarding, pausing. Asking myself thee same questions. Did I make big blunder? I should have stayed back in Delhi?

I should have done something? I should have said something?

Night came, midnight came, morning came, but my answers did not.

I dragged myself to thee loo, got ready fast-fast and then made second mistake. Of not calling Dumpy immediately. First mistake was agreeing to go to Bathinda with his Combo Pack.

Irresponsible fellow was missing till nine o clock. I called and called him, but got only Airtel girl on thee line. 'Number you're calling is switched off.' By thee time, I heard his car horn, my thermometer's mercury was touching sky.

HONK!HONK!

Keep maaroing horn, I boiled, refusing to get up.

BEEP!BEEP!

Keep calling cell, I steamed, refusing to pick up.

TING TONG! TING TONG!

Keep bajaoing doorbell, I fried, refusing to step out.

KNOCK!KNOCK!

'Where were you, *maa ke* @#$% –' I opened thee door.

And found Mummyji standing there in her nightie, dupatta forming V on chest.

I don't know who was more shockum-shocked, she or me.

Hai, how did I know Sukhna would be sleeping and Mummyji awake? She was thee Sleeping Beauty of Ahluwali House. Her (non-kitty) mornings started at 10 o' clock.

'I thought Sukhna had opened main door…thought it was that Dumpy knocking,' I said, PMS (oho, Please Mistake Sorry) expression on my face. 'Ok, ta ta bye bye. See you.'

I picked up my Louis Vuitton bag (two thousand rupees only, from Dumpy Da Swag) and ran to thee main door without waiting for her reply.

Dumpy, Simran, Yograj were standing outside, leaning against Dumpy's family car. Thee car was like Dumpy Da Swag products – Ford Endeavor, but with BMW symbol. (Dumpy's Honda City also had four bangle – oho, Audi – symbol.)

'What, *yaar*, Mahi,' Dumpy complained. 'How many times I rang thee door. Your ting-tong not working or what?'

'Your ding-dong's working, *na*, then be quiet!'

3

In which a long drives turns into the longest drive of the heroine's life

PHATTTTT!

Raj and Simran's mouths fell to thee ground.

I gave them 'Ya, I'm like this only, what you'll do' look.

Dumpy burst out laughing. 'Oh Mahi, you're too much!'

'I'm three much,' I said, walking to thee backseat. 'Now can we go? Or you want to be more late?'

'You remember Simran and Raj?' Dumpy asked, going to thee driver side.

'Simran and Raj? From *Dilwale Dulhania Le Jayenge*?' I asked innocently.

'No, no, Simran and Raj from Model Town, Ludhiana.'

'Oh.'

We did Hello, How are you, Nice to meet you.

'Please excuse, Mahi,' Raj said urgently, 'but can I use your toilet?'

'NO!' Dumpy, Simran and I answered at thee same time.

'Didn't you go at Dumpy's house?' Sister asked brother.

Brother did mumble-mumble and avoided looking at me. I turned my face. As if I wanted to hear details of his *susu* times.

'You can have thee front seat,' Simran said as I reached for thee back door. 'You're senior to us, after all.'

Hai, I *toh* felt like Kareena when Alia said Kareena was her senior in film industry. Fully insulted.

'I'm twenty-six,' I said in rough voice.

'I'm twenty-one,' Simran informed, getting inside. 'So is Raj...'

Then what? Her twin brother would be eighty-one?

'By thee time I was twenty-one, I'd already started Ludhiana to London,' I said softly like I was remembering thee good old time. Actually, I was maaroing her taunt crisper than Ludhiana winter. College was over months back, but Madam was still thinking 'What to do next'. Jobless!

Raj went running to hold front door open for me like he was my personal driver.

'Did you know we're twins?' Simran asked.

'I didn't know,' I said.

'What you didn't know?' Dumpy said, getting into driver seat. 'I told you, Mahi, thee first time you met Simran-Raj in my house.'

'Our Mummyji also has memory problem,' Simran said understandingly. 'Happens with age.'

Kutti! Talking as if I was hundred year old with legs dangloing in grave.

Before I could give matching reply, she took out her cell phone and started going *click! click! click!*

'Come, come, come, let's all take selfies.'

'I don't take selfies,' I growled.

Not early in thee morning. Not after spending sleepless night. Not looking like one horror film.

For thee next few minutes, there were only clickum-click sounds in thee car.

Suddenly, Simran went squeal-squeal, 'Oh, ladoo, open your top no, please, please.'

'You want me to open my shirt, barfi?' Dumpy replied in same lovey-dovey voice.

Uff! I *toh* felt like I was watching shooting of *Love in Haldiram.*

'Not that top, naughty boy,' Simran went giggle giggle, 'top top.' She pointed to car's sun roof.

She wanted our heads to fly off in the heat or what?

I used my senior citizen veto power. 'No.'

'Please.'

'No means no.'

She made *'huhn'* sound, crossed her arms and sat back in seat with bugged face.

'Oh, jalebi, don't be sad,' Dumpy cooed like pigeon. 'Here, take, take,' He reached for one button.

SWISHHHHH!

Sun roof opened, Simran jumped up like excited puppy, her head disappeared.

'Wooooo! Wooooo! I love wind hitting my face.'

I *toh* wanted to hit her face thee same way.

'Raj, come and join me.'

'I'm fine here,' Raj replied.

'Dumpy, you come.'

It was Dumpy, not Shaktimaan. As if he could drive and put head in sun roof at thee same time. *Khotti!*

'Mahi Didi, you –'

'STOP THEE CAR!' I shouted.

Dumpy turned to look at me with concern. 'What? What? What happened?'

'STOP! CAR! NOW!'

Dumpy braked and his tyres – means, his car tyres – went screech-screech.

'Hello, thee name is Mahi!' I told Headless Body firmly. 'M-A-H-I, Mahi. Got it? Not Mahi Didi. No one calls me Didi. Not even my little brother Nikku.'

'Sorry, Didi...I mean, sorry, Mahi,' Simran's headless body replied. 'I was going to call Behenji, but I thought...'

Oh! *toh* MJ (not Michael Jackson, Madam Jobless) could think also?

There was silence in thee car for few minutes.

'Idea!' Headless body spoke again. 'Let's all play *antakshari*!'

We were going in school bus or what?

'Come, let's play, please,' she begged.

She started singing that irritating *antakshari* song, but stopped in thee middle. 'You first, Mahi. Sing song starting with M.'

'I don't sing.'

'What? You don't sing also?'

My teeth went grind-grind. First, she made me sound like hundred-year-old *buddhi*. Then she made me sound like hundred-percent bore. Bore *buddhi* Mahi leaned forward to touch button and close thee sun roof, cutting Simran's body and head into two pieces. Unluckily, Dumpy caught my hand. He moved his lips 'Please please please' and made 'Be nice to my GF' face.

I took long loud deep breaths. Control, Mahi, control.

But I couldn't control. Because Headless Body called out, 'What are those sounds, Mahi? Are you okay?'

I was thee oppo-site of okay. I'd headache, body ache, back pain, leg pain...*Hai*, it suddenly strike to me. I *toh* had become my stepmother! So many health problems, all at thee same time.

'Please stop stop stop,' Raj said suddenly.

'What happened to *you* now?' Dumpy asked.

'Please, personal reason,' Raj said with too much pain in his voice.

'He has to go to toilet again,' Headless Body answered.

I was thinking that Raj was adult man with baby's bladder, when Headless Body explained, 'Last night party, too much beer.'

'Next time wear adult diaper,' I told him sternly.

And immediately thought of thee person who used to say that. Lavith. I didn't want to think of him, but I was helpless from habit. Everything reminded me of him.

'Let's see what's coming on radio,' Dumpy said.

'How can you "see" what's coming? It's radio, not TV,' Headless Body went chuckle-chuckle.

Love love love love love hua...

Hai, whole world was doing conspiracies against me.

It was my pet name for Him. Not ladoo, barfi, rabdi, kulfi. Short, sweet, to thee point. Lav.

I gave one slap to radio button and changed thee channel.

Love me love me love me Mama says you love me...

I hit thee stupid radio button again.

Don't know whose face I saw in thee morning, I grumbled inside.

As if she could hear me, person whose face I saw in thee morning WhatsApped.

BEEP!

Bhooto: Reached? Arre, we were going in car not jumbo jet.

Mahi: No.

Bhooto: Then when will you reach? I was not Bejan Daruwala. I couldn't predict thee future.

Mahi: When we reach, I'll tell.

Bhooto: Don't forget to call. Last time you forgot.

Mahi: Last time?

Bhooto: College trip, you promised to call, but forgot.

Uff! College was 6 years back.

I closed my eyes, but my head started eating circles.

'Stop thee car,' I said weakly.

'Now what happened?' Dumpy asked. 'Did anyone call her Didi in their mind? Ha ha ha.'

I made loud vomiting sound and quickly covered my mouth with my hand.

Dumpy looked scared means scared. 'OKAY, OKAY, OKAY, I'M STOPPING...PLEASE DON'T....NO *ULTI*....NOT IN MY CAR...PLEASE!'

The second he braked, I kicked thee door open and went running to thee roadside bushes. And decorated them.

Dumpy and Raj came running behind me.

'Are you okay?' Simran's Bodyless Head asked from thee sun roof.

I was okay. Roadside bushes were not.

'I know why,' Dumpy accused me. 'You didn't have break-fast. Correct? You should always eat before road trip, travel on full stomach –'

'Bloody don't start your lecture now...*cough cough*...'

I took mineral water bottle from Raj and poured it on my face like model in Bisleri ad.

'We'll get breakfast in Andeep's house?' Bodyless
Head asked when we walked back to thee car.

'Breakfast? We'll get full-on attitude,' I grumbled.

Just because they were thee boy side, they thought
they could show *tevar* (oho, act smart). I was going to
give them solid...

As if she could hear my thoughts, Dingy
WhatsApped.

BEEP!

Dingy: Mahi, please don't create scene there.

Mahi: You want to get married?

Dingy: Yes.

Mahi: To Andeep?

Dingy: Yes.

Mahi: In Bangkok?

Dingy: Yes.

Mahi: Then let me do what I want.

Dingy: Okay. But don't create scene there.

Uff! No trust only. When Veeru sent Jai with his
proposal to Mausiji, did he spoon feed? No, *ji*, not.
Veeru was mouthshut.com. Jai did what he wanted.
And everyone was happy. Producer, audience, Veeru-
Basanti. All because friend trusted friend.

I *toh* was so bugged, I switched off myself and cell
both for rest of thee journey. Got up only when we got
to Andeep's house.

Dulhe Raja came running out of house, looking like
tension case.

'Please excuse,' Raj asked urgently. 'But can I use
your toilet?'

'NO!' Dumpy, Simran and I shouted at thee same time.

'You got Dingy's WhatsApp, Mahi?'

Then only I realised. Dingy was only mouthpiece,
Andeep was thee criminal mastermind.

I lifted one hand like politician and marched inside. Ludhiana Brigade followed me like Vodafone dog.

After their engagement, I was coming to thee zoo only now. This time also I got same thought – if Maneka Gandhi saw Andeep's house what would happen? Each wall had head of some dead animal. Each floor has skin of some dead animal.

Thee big sofa had bodies of two alive animals. They were stuffing face. Instead of getting up and saying 'come come', they just waved us inside. Like they were cinema-hall ticket-checkers.

Male animal caught Dumpy's hands before they reached his feet. Like he was going to touch thee feet. *Arre*, who bends down-down-down and touches feet nowadays? Thee trend is to stop half-way and touch something else (knees, baba, knees).

Female animal wiped hand on our heads when we bent down to do PP (not pee, *Pairi Paina* – oho, touching feet).

'Sorry, knees troubling too much,' Auntyji gave excuse for not getting up.

Uncleji didn't even bother to do that.

Raj, who was twisting his body like Shammi Kapoor in one of his hit songs, couldn't control.

'Uncleji-Auntyji if he cannot use your toilet, he'll use your carpet,' Simran said in warning *wala* voice.

Uncleji-Auntyji's backsides flew up few inches from thee sofa.

'Sit, sit, Uncleji-Auntyji,' Dumpy said. 'We'll take him to toilet,' Dumpy offered.

'Bladder problem,' I explained, after thee Three Idiots had left. I sat on thee sofa next to thee stuffed tiger. Oho, to show I was no less.

'Uncleji-Auntyji, I'll not beat around your bushes...'

Uncleji, who was sitting with shutter open, quickly closed his knees.

'...I'll come straight to thee point. It's Dingy dream to have destination wedding...Bangkok's best of both thee worlds, cheap and close by...don't worry, you don't have to lift one finger also...I'll take care of everything. Except finance, ha ha ha.'

One small boy flew into thee room. In Andeep's house everything was too extreme. Last time, there was senior citizen (older than Simran had made me sound) serving. This time, child labour.

'Limca, where you'd died? How many times I called you,' Auntyji scolded him.

I looked at Limca and licked my lips. He was carrying tray with three glasses of lassi on it.

I badly needed drink. My throat was all scratch-scratch from vomitting-shomitting.

Limca kept thee tray on centre table. Uncleji leaned forward, picked up first glass and drank it fully. Then he picked up second glass and finished that. Then it was Auntyji's turn. She reached for the third glass and finished it in ten seconds flat.

I turned to look at thee Man of thee Moment, who was sitting quiet like some sant (not perfume, saint).

'Andeep?' I gave him the same look Betaal gave Vikram. Speak or I'll make *keema* out of you.

In reply, Andeep turned his back to me, reached for glass of water lying on side table and gulpoed it down. He drank so fast that he started choking.

Auntyji jumped up from sofa like bread slice from toaster and started doing *dham! dham! dham!* on his backside.

'Andeep?' I tried again after cough and Auntiji both calmed down.

In reply, he coughed. First silently. Then softly. Then chokingly. Bloody two-face. Outside his house, he roamed like Singh is King, inside his house like Manmohan Singh. I wanted to give him BPL (not electronics, *Bum Pe Laat*). Oho, Kick on thee backside.

'It's thee question of our only son's marriage, you know,' Uncleji said, puffing up like poori in oil.

I know, Uncle, I wanted to reply. That I was cent-percent correct in calling Andeep *khotte da puttar*. Son of ass (not bum, donkey).

Typical mentality. Just like Bhooto wanted to do full *vasooli* at hotels, these types of people wanted to do full *paisa vasool* at son's wedding. *Arre*, it was marriage not money-back offer. Third-rate people. First-class *kameenas*!

4

In which the Bangkok Battalion goes down fighting

Control Mahi control, I told myself. I took deep yoga breaths before opening mouth. 'Uncleji-Auntyji, I'm not only your B2B's BFF–'

'What?' Auntyji sat up straight in sofa like I was narrating Ramayan in Tamil.

'Bahu 2 Be's Best Friend Forever,' Andeep explained, at last breaking his vow of silence.

Oh, *toh* now your tongue's back in your mouth? I wanted to ask.

Somehow I stopped myself and started searching my handbag for my visiting card. I pulled it out like it was my sword and put it under their noses. 'I'm also top *ka* party-planner.'

'Ludhina to London,' Auntiji said, reading thee card aloud. 'Panty planners.'

'That's printing mistake,' I said, quickly snatching it from her fingers. I stuffed thee sword back into my LV, blowing out frustoo breath. Some people had no value for talent.

'All that's okay,' Uncleji spoke up. 'But do you have any experience in planning big-big weddings?'

Oh Uncleji, I wanted to reply, what experience you needed to have your *laudu* son?

'Uncleji, I shouldn't say from my own mouth. But you can ask anyone. I'm thee most experienced girl in whole of Ludhiana!'

It was truth. LTL had been rocking-shocking in thee last six years.

For thee next few minutes, I gave full status update of my business. From birthday party to condolence meet, from wedding reception to golden jubilee celebration, from bachelor night to break-up bash, from kitty get-together to kirtan gathering, from school reunion to sundowner, I recited all thee events we'd handled in one breath like Udipi waiter.

I paused to catch breath and looked at thee people I was serving.

But they didn't look impressed one bit with thee items on my menu.

Suddenly, Auntyji lifted her head and let out loud howl like wolf. 'OYEEEEEEE! LIMCAAAA! LIMCA!'

All heads swung to thee right as if they were expecting Limca bottle to come flying out of thee kitchen.

'He's gone deaf I think so,' Auntyji said, jumping to her feet with energy of sixteen-year-old. 'Told him to get halwa...'

She jogged off towards the kitchen, forgetting that her knees were supposed to be troubling her.

I took yoga breath, ran my fingers through my bra-length hairss, before turning to Uncelji. 'Uncleji, you should be happy it's Bangkok and not some bore *sa* place,' I said jokily even though I was mood out. 'Imagine all thee fun-shun you'll have....'

Funny look came into Uncleji's eyes.

Hai, he *toh* was imagining *that* type fun. Perverted old man! If he wasn't Dingy's father-in-law, I'd have made him straight.

Luckily, Auntyji came back in time, interrupting his wet daydreams. She was followed by Limca. This time, he was carrying silver tray with three halwa bowls on it.

I licked my lips. I badly needed food. My stomach was all grumble-grumble.

'What are you staring at my face?' Auntyji scolded him. 'Put them down.'

Limca put thee bowls on centre table.

Auntyji picked up thee first bowl and passed it to Uncleji. Uncleji's hand disappeared into thee bowl and cleaned it in one minute flat. He burped in satisfaction, wiping his hand on his beard.

Auntyji was not far behind. She pounced on thee second bowl, then thee third. By thee time she was done, bowls looked like thee utensils in Vim Bar ads. *Chakachak* clean, ting!

Good, I thought, poor Limca's work was saved. He didn't have to wash them. I was imagining calling thee labour department and getting Uncleji and Auntyji arrested, but Auntyji punctured my thought balloon.

'But what about expenses?' she asked, placing thee empty bowls back on thee centre table.

'What for you? As if you have to pay from your own pocket...'

That's it. Andeep started looking like bride who found out groom had erection problems on wedding night.

If we were in Hindi movie, tension type music would have started. *Dhan te nan.* If we were in Hindi serial, I'd have turned face three times. *Dhanan dhanan dhanan.*

Andeep's eyes and lips and hands were silently crying PLEASE.

I counted till ten – in English and Hindi and Punjabi – and somehow forced myself to change my expression. Gave my most special smile. Spoke in my sweetest voice. 'What I mean to say, Dingy's parents will spare no expense to make wedding super-duper hit, *ji*. Trust me, thee whole world is having destination wedding. You just come and have fun. Bangkok style.' I was so despo, I winked. Just to convince at least one party.

'We're not that modern-shodern,' Auntyji said. 'Plus, we're calling more than thousand people…'

Arre, it was wedding or politician's rally?

'…how can we take so many guests to Bangkok…'

'You really want to call so many guests, Uncleji? They will only come for free food. You can cut off thee extra names from your guest list –'

'No extra-vextra,' he interrupted me. 'We've gone and eaten in everyone's wedding, now it's their turn. We have to repay.'

Repay with another person's money. Why not!

I was ready to hit them with Number Two (not shit, option). 'You can keep thee reception in Bathinda and repay.'

'No, no. We're calling limited crowd for reception. No need to feed them again-again.'

I looked at Andeep. Andeep looked at thee Three Idiots who had returned.

All three were doing *hee hee* as if they had won big fort in some bloody battle.

Dumpy looked at my face and his smile went *phurrr*.

I'd tried my best to change Uncleji Auntyji's mind. But they were like retired politicians in government bungalows. Stuckum-stuck.

Bas, I put my hands up. We all put our bums up.

'You're not going to stay for lunch?' Auntyji asked with *faku* sadness.

No, because you both will finish that also, I replied inside-inside.

We took blessings from Uncleji's Auntyji's halwa hands and did bye-shyes.

'Where are we going for lunch?' Simran asked thee minute we got into car.

I threw her 'GO DIE' look. Her BF's sister's dream was broken and she wanted to build stomach lining.

'Let's go to Facebook Da Dhabba,' Dumpy suggested, winning same look from me.

My blood was boiling. He was least bothered about his own flesh and blood. He'd lost his heart and his senses.

'Yummy,' Simran licked her lips. 'Mummy, I'm so hungry.'

Bas, Dumpy started driving as if he was in Formula One race, doing competition with that famous driver, what's his name...Shoemaker, Showmaker, something.

'DUMPY!' I shouted as he almost hit one bullock on thee road.

'*Bechari* Simran is hungry,' he answered.

'Bitch-ari Simran,' I repeated in acid voice. Only she could insult me or what?

Forget Shoemaker, Dumpy took us to thee Dhabba faster than jumbo jet. Simran gave thee order faster than our backsides touched the charpoy.

'Let's get back home soon,' Raj said, stuffing choley into his mouth fast.

'You've appointment with Prime Minster?' I asked in Dabur honey voice.

'Whole country has appointment with Prime Minster,' he chomp-chomped. 'Don't you know he's coming on TV tonight to talk to thee nation?'

He's coming on TV, not to your house for tea, I wanted to bark. But my mouth was full. Plus, I was full mood out.

'Must be something important...' Raj continued, tearing his butter naan with both hands like it was paper. 'Actually, Mahi, I wanted to talk to you about something important...' he stopped and gave me shy type look.

TOINGGGGG!

My eyebrows went up and mixed with my hairs. I knew it! I knew he'd got thee hots for me. Oho, it was thee way he'd been looking at me. With painful, constipated, helpless expression. As if he was trying very hard to get something out, but failing to do so. But thee long drive to Bathinda had acted like laxative and his feelings were ready to come out.

'Please Raj,' I said, staring at my plate. 'I don't want to hear it.'

'Please, Mahi, you won't regret...'

I was regretting. Talking to him. Sitting in car with him. I hadn't given him grass, but I should have kept distance from him. God only knew what romantic pulao he was cooking in his head, with me as thee main ingredient.

'Please, Mahi,' he begged. 'I know you need someone badly.'

I used to think like that, too. That I needed someone in life. That I needed love. That I needed Lavith. But I'd learned Life's Number One lesson thee hard way. In this world, we're all alone. We come alone, live alone, and bloody die alone.

'I don't need anyone,' I said, pushing away my plate. My hunger died seeing thee hungry expression on Raj's face. I blushed from top to toes. *Hai*, some people had no control over their emotions.

'Just give me one chance,' he please-pleased. 'Promise I won't disappoint.'

'You're disappointing me now itself…you're much-much younger than me.'

'So what? Age doesn't matter. I don't have much experience, but I'll do my very best to satisfy you…'

I sprang up like mattress. Perverted boy!

'What's wrong with you, Raj?' I shouted. Small pieces of tandoori roti went flying from my mouth on to Raj's face. He wiped them away with middle finger. 'Did you take cocaine-shocaine in Andeep's toilet?'

'No! Never! I swear, I swear I don't touch drugs!' Raj replied, jumping up too.

'You can take them without touching,' I said. I wanted to give him back-hand slap. I somehow controlled and used back-hand to wipe oil from my mouth.

'I don't have any bad habits, Mahi. You can ask anyone for my *bio data*.'

'I don't want your bloody *bio data*,' I snapped, looking around for something to wipe my hands.

Raj pulled out white hanky from his pocket and offered.

I hesitated. But then I thought, I was accepting hanky, not his hand. I took it and cleaned my fingers till white hanky became brown hanky.

'Is it because of some bad experience? That's why you don't want to take second chance?' Raj asked, twisting his hands.

What could I say? No, no, it's because I love someone else? So I jumped on thee excuse. 'Ya, that's why.'

Dumpy, who was eating quietly till now, spoke up.

'When did you have bad experience? You've never kept assistant before.'

'You shut up, you don't know anything—' I barked, before applying sudden brakes on my mouth. 'Assistant???'

'Yes, assistant,' Dumpy informed. 'he's applying for your assistant's job.'

Why, what you thought?' Simran, who was eating more than thee truck drivers on thee next table, asked in sly voice.

Hai, I *toh* turned water-water from embarrassment. Raj did want to join with me, but only in business. He did want to satisfy me, but like good professional. Simply I'd called him perverted.

I covered my red cheeks with my dupatta and cleared my throat. 'Yes, yes, I'd hired one assistant... many months back...very bad she was...liar, thief, cheater, druggie —'

'What? Who? When?' Dumpy pounced on me. 'You never told me. Even Dingy didn't open her mouth.'

Loose mouth *laudu*! Couldn't keep his mouth shut.

'We don't tell you all thee inside details of our business,' I sniffed, handing Raj back his brown hanky.

'But Dingy's getting married,' Dumpy insisted. 'How will you manage? Won't you need help?'

'No,' I said firmly.

'Why?'

Because it was my business, my wish, my life. What for him? If he was so bothered, why didn't he give Raj a job?

'Please, Mahi, give me job. I'll give you my all.'

Forget all, I didn't even want him this much.

'Thank you for offer, Raj, but I work alone…'

'That's true,' Dumpy nodded, 'She's Hunterwali plus Revolver Rani…all in one…'

Simran covered her mouth with one hand and started giggling.

I gave Dumpy 'You are finished, *kutte*' look.

'If you've finished *thoosoing* your face,' I said, looking at Simran. 'And you've finished giving *bio-data*,' I added, looking at Raj. 'Can we bloody leave?'

5

In which the heroine comes face to face with her past

I was flying across seven seas for thee first time.

I was so excited, so excited, don't ask. Thought I'd chill, do *masti*, watch free movies, eat free food like pig on thee flight. But when kismet is *gaandu*, what will do *paandu*? Oho, when luck itself is bad, what you'll do.

First, I couldn't watch one movie also.

Other passengers put seat belt after they sat down, but Mahi? She puts on thee ear phones. So I put ear phones on ears and fingered thee screen. Once, twice, thrice. No reaction. Blank it stayed. I thought it was like my washing machine. It'd work only after getting one tight slap. I was about to give it one shot, when thee air-hostess came and said, 'The flight entertainment system is down, Ma'am.'

My mood went down from there.

Second, leave seeing movie, I only saw next seat passenger getting drunkum-drunk.

He even had thee guts to ask me, 'Madam, you're not drinking. Can you get one Red Label for me?' When air-hostess came, I asked her. But not for drink. For change of seat. But thee flight was full, so I was stuck in Bewafa Bar with Devdas.

Third, bloody flight was late. It was night by thee time I took boat from Bangkok Airport and reached Hawa-Hawai island. Oho, that was not thee name of the island. It was thee name I remembered.

On top of that, I got stuck with *kambakht* taxi driver. He took me for full Island Darshan. Round and round we went around same area. Third time when we passed thee same restaurant, I became like Mentos ad. My brain's light got switched on.

I told him in Indian don voice that if he didn't take me to thee correct place immediately, I'd give him solid. *Bas*, in five minutes flat, I was outside Rembrandt Resort.

'Oh, Lem-la,' he said, reading thee board outside. 'Why you not tell?'

Arre, how I could tell 'Lemla' when thee name was Rembrandt?

I was tired means tired. I dragged myself and my strolley to thee reception.

'*Swadeekha!*' called out thee man at reception.

He had round face, thin *hair*s, thick specs, and he was smiling like he was Vicco-Vajradanti model. He looked like hero of those kung-fu shung-fu, karate-sharate movies that Niku used to watch non-stop in olden days. What was his name...Chusli or Guthli or something.

He came from behind thee counter and put seashell garland around my neck.

Before I could say, 'Thank you, Mr. Chusli', two slim-trim girls popped up from behind thee counter like popcorns from microwave. They did some steps like they were waving mosquitoes away (I think so Thai people called it dancing).

Before I could tell Deepika-Anushka, 'Come to Punjab, I show you real thing', another man popped up from behind the counter, holding welcome drink. I took XL coconut from XS tray and looked behind him. But there were no more people in thee welcoming committee.

Chusli joined his hands and bent down. 'Welcome to Hua Hin island. Welcome to Lembla Resort.'

I joined my hands and bent down.

They smiled at me. I smiled at them. They smiled more. Then I got worried they were expecting tip. I quickly made O with left hand to show lock. I put right finger inside it to make key-inside-lock action. And then I asked, 'Where?'

'Haw' expression came on all their faces.

I was confused. Then only I remembered Bangkok was Sex Capital of world. *Hai*, they thought I was asking where I could go for bang-bang! As if I was some sex criminal foreign tourist.

'No, no, not like that!' I said quickly, doing the key action alone. 'Key, key.'

Relief came on their faces. 'Aah, key,' Chusli went behind counter and handed me card.

'Your loom may alive, Madame,' Chusli smiled.
Hain?

'Loom may? Alive?' I asked, confused.

He nodded.

I *toh* needed subtitles to understand him. Then it striked to me. 'Oh, loom mate. You mean, my roommate has arrived.'

'Yes, loom may alive,' he confirmed.

Andeep's big sis, Gurdeep, was coming from Mumbai. We both were going to make thee arrangements. Gurdeep didn't know P of party-planning. But what to do. Dingy was bride and busy. Ten thousand things she had to do back in Ludhiana. And *laudu* Andeep's parents said they wanted someone to help me. My shoe, help me. They wanted someone to keep eye on me and thee budget. *Huhn!*

'Wedding advisol will meet you tomolo.'

'Wedding advisor will meet me tomorrow?

Oho, I didn't need any wedding advisor-shadvisor. But resort was giving him free – means, part of thee package. So I thought what goes for me, let him come.

'Good stay,' Chusli bent down and folded hands.

'This way,' the other man bent down and picked up handle of my strolley.

I followed him out of thee Reception hut, taking deep breath. Thee resort was even more beautiful in offline.

I'd seen online. Eleven rooms. All in different-different styles. Thai, English, Arabian and what not. Thanks to God, Andeep – means, his Delhi contacts had booked it. First time in his life he did something useful.

We passed landscape garden, swimming pool, gym, library, children's play area, riverside verandah restaurant, and then we reached thee room.

I took card with thanks, put it in slot, turned door handle softly and tippy-toed inside. Room was dark. Only Gurdeep's bedside lamp was on. She was fast asleep on one side of bed. Blanket was covering her fully like she was dead body in morgue.

I didn't want to disturb. Softly and silently, I grabbed thee bath gown lying on my side of thee bed, got out of my salwar-kameez and collapsed. I was so tired, so tired, I slept like *this*.

God only knows how long I slept. I was forced to wake up when sun rays fell on my face. I didn't feel like opening my eyes. My chest felt heavy. As if someone had placed heavy stone on it. Bets, it was that fish on thee flight.

But suddenly, stone on my chest moved! My eyes flew open and I looked down.

There was hand on my chest! Hand was big! Hand was brown! Hand was *hairy!*

There was man in thee room. In thee bed.

'AAAAAAAAAAAAAAAAAAAAAAAAA!' I yelled at thee top of my lungs, throwing hand off my chest like it was poisonous snake, and jumping off thee bed. I looked around like mad bull, and grabbed thee first thing I saw. Thee big lamp on thee side table. I gave one big pull and it came in my hand with shade, wire and plug. I threw it full force on thee blanket on thee man on thee bed.

'AAAAAAAAAAAAAAAAAAAAAAAA!' Thee man screamed as if thee lamp had hit him on his ding dong really badly. Thee blanket went up flying, man attached to thee hand came out and...

And I died.

It was not man! It was – *HAYO RABBA* – Lavith! My past love Lavith. My ex-BF Lavith. Topless Lavith. Big brown chest. Big brown shoulders. Big brown biceps. Same black eyes. Same black beard. Same black *chaddi*.

His *chaddi* still had magnet powers. *ZOINKKKKKK!* My eyes went and got stuck to them. I hoped I hadn't injured his private part – means, the lamp hadn't injured his private part. It was his fault that he was inside thee room. But what had his poor ding-dong done to me? Means, it had done many things in thee past, but what was its fault now? Why should it get injured for no reason?

Suddenly, old English movie I'd seen came inside my head. In which heroine said that whenever you see your ex-lover after long time, first thing that comes to your mind is thee last time you had humpy-pumpy. Our last session came in front of my eyes. Rainy night, big fight...

'Mahendar!' he exclaimed, breaking my daydream.

Thee last session went *phurrr* out of my mind. Leaving smoke coming out of my ears.

Just like I called him names – Luv, Luvee and Tarzan (because he looked like grown up Mowgli), he called me names (Baby, Ma-hee and Mahendar Singh Dhoni (because like MSD, I was always in form, hitting fours and sixes).

'Some things never change,' he cluck-clucked.

I was so shockum-shocked, not one word came out of my mouth.

He was meeting me after almost two months. But instead of looking angry, upsetted, hurted, he was looking least bothered. And that made me angry, upsetted, hurted.

'Where's Gurdeep?' I barked, looking around thee room like one mad.

He looked inside his blanket. 'Not here.'

'I know she's not there,' I growled. 'She's married.'

'I don't have a problem with that,' he replied with wolfy smile.

'Hello, not every girl wants to do *chak dhoom dhoom* with you –'

'Well, that girl did,' he pointed behind me.

I turned around like one donkey and saw myself in thee mirror on thee wall looking like Santa (not Banta's friend, Claus). White bath gown, red face.

Before I could say something, he pulled thee blanket off and got out of thee bed. *Hai*, my tongue also got out. Seeing him in those black-shack, mini-shini, satin-watin *chaddis* again…

Control, Mahi, control, I told myself desperately. But there was no use. I stared at him like he was heroine in wet-white-saree-under-waterfall and I was Shakti Kapoor. Like he was deep-fried pakora and I was size-zero model. Like he was full-marks and I was three-time-fail student.

'Wow!' Tarzan whistled. 'Never thought I'd live to see the day. Mahendar the Great at a loss for words.'

'What are you doing in my room?' I asked, hissing like cobra snake.

'Your room? If I remember correctly, there was no one in the room when I checked in.'

'So?'

'So, how in fuck's name is it *your* room?'

'Listen, you,' I said, pointing finger at him. 'I can also use bad words –'

He held up his left hand. 'Sure you can. I mean, you're a pro at it. What's the latest on that front, by the way?'

I gave him blank look.

'What's the latest – he broke off to make quotation marks – "bad" word you're tripping on?'

I hadn't played with uncooked marbles in life. I knew what he was doing. He was trying to provoke me.

'Me and bad word?' I said innocently.

He went on like he'd not heard me. 'The last creative cuss word I'd learnt was what…' he clicked his fingers, hunting for thee word in his mind, '*chutiyam* sulphide?'

'Sulphate,' I corrected him automatically.

'Gotcha!' he said like he'd won major victory in life.

Saala!

Like smart hunter, he'd set trap and I'd walked into it.

'Anyways,' I said, marching to other corner of thee room, where his suitcase was. I gave it one solid kick. 'This is my room. So, please, pack up and get thee hell out.'

He folded his arms over his chest, looking like Rana Dagubatti in *Bahubali*. 'Like hell I will. You've got a problem, you leave.'

'I can't,' I said proudly. 'I'm thee official wedding planner.'

'So am I.'

I grunted like pig. 'Funny joke! I didn't know you could plan weddings.'

'There are lots of things you don't know about me.'

'I know that you're investment banker working in –'

'I quit,' he told me.

Haw expression came to my face.

'Told ya,' he said as if he'd won major victory, 'there are lotsa things you don't know about me.'

And I don't want to, I wanted to bark. But I didn't want to make him bigger enemy. I knew why he was here. Purposely. To provoke me. To take *badla* on me. I'd ditched him and he was thirsty for revenge like *bhatakti aatma* (oho, restless ghost).

Hai, I *toh* panicked. He'd found only Dingy's wedding to take revenge on me?

I took deep breath and used my compromise voice. 'I know you're holding big grudge against me. But what has poor Dingy done? Why are you doing this to her?'

'Grudge, what grudge?' he asked. 'And what am I doing?'

He walked up to thee coffee-maker, not bothering to pull up his *chaddi* which was hanging down like mango from low branch. I was getting high looking at it. I had to, *had to* tear my eyes away and concentrate on what he was saying.

'...Gurdeep couldn't make it...her mom-in-law's down with dengue or was that malaria... anyway, whatever...Uncleji wanted someone to represent the boy's side. Andeep asked me, I agreed. It's as simple as that...'

Simple? Thee situation was more complicated than that movie Aamir Khan's wife made – what was its name... Dhobi Shobi something.

Tarzan switched on thee coffee-maker. Saliva almost leaked from my mouth. Anyone who knew Mahi Ahluwalia one percent also, *na*, knew that I hated making things. And he knew me more than one percent. Still, he made only one cup and walked off to other side of thee room.

Kutta!

'Please...'

His ears went up like dog's. 'Wow! Are you feeling quite all right –?'

There's nothing wrong with my health, I wanted to shout.

'Did you actually use the "P" word? Are you pleading with me, Mahendar?'

'You want me to stop?' I gave warning.

'Not at all, please continue,' he said, dropping down *phattt* on thee sofa. 'I've a feeling I'm going to enjoy this very much.'

I peesoed my teeth and continued. 'Look, Lavith –'

'That sounded odd,' he cut in.

I was confused. 'What?'

'The way you pronounced my name. If I remember correctly, you used to place more emphasis on "Lav"...'

I became redder than red chilli powder.

'...Or maybe I'm wrong,' he went on talking. 'Maybe this is exactly how you pronounced it...maybe I'm just imagining things...after all, it's been, what, one-and-half months?'

One month, three weeks, two days, I corrected inside my head.

'Forget about all that,' I said outside, before he could say one more word. 'That's history.'

'You know what they say about history...' he began.

'What?'

'It repeats itself,' he finished with *paaji* (not elder, wicked) smile.

My heart was like Tiger (not animal, Shroff). It was dancing like anything inside, but outside, I was like Arjun Rampal. Expressionless.

'In this case, it won't repeat,' I said in firm voice, making my shoulders straight.

He got up and started walking towards me. He came and stood so close to me, I could smell his P (not *susu*, perfume).

'Sure about that?' He asked, tightly locking his eyes on me.

Bas, my heart started dancing like Tiger Shroff's big daddy (not Jackie Shroff, Prabhudeva). My mouth started feeling like dry-shy. My hand started feeling wet-shet. My skin started feeling tingly-mingly.

He bent his head. Slowly but surely, his mouth started coming near mine. One more second, and I was going to jump on him like Bhooto jumps on non-veg after keeping fast.

TING TONG!TING TONG!

My brain that had gone *phusss*, came back to life. I pushed him away and ran to thee toilet, locked thee door and leaned against thee basin, hand on chest. It was running faster than deers escaping cheetah.

I heard him go to thee door. I strained my ears, but couldn't hear anything. I was already inside bathroom, so why not take shower, I thought. I pulled thee belt of my bathrobe and was about to slide it down from my shoulders.

'You know I can see you from here, right?' Tarzan called out in lazy voice.

I jumped up like bread from toaster. Bathroom had window! It was open! It was too much!

He went chuckle-chuckle before calling out, 'I'm going to the Reception. Will see what can be done about our, um, situation.'

DHADAAAAAAMMM!

Thee door closed behind him.

I waited for few seconds to make sure he was actually gone. Then I came out of thee bathroom and collapsed on thee bed. I gave lakh-lakh thanks to God for thee doorbell. Or God only knew what I'd have done – oho, why to lie, I knew what I'd have done.

Hai, where only I got stuck. I thought, slapping my forehead.

Everything was going A-okay. Uncelji Auntyji had said 'No Never'. Thee wedding was going to be in Bathinda. Everyone (except Dingy) was happy. I was planning thee wedding in style.

But now I was standing in bath gown in Hawa-Hawai island with Tarzan ready to drink my blood.

It was all Andeep's fault. No, it was Dingy's fault. No, it was thee government's fault.

I went inside flashback.

6

The one where the government pours water over the heroine's plans

Driving back from Bathinda, I was water-water with shame. I'd failed in thee most important exam. Exam of life. I'd promised to gift Dingy Bangkok bang-bang, but could only give her bore Bathinda first night.

After Dumpy, Simran and Raj dropped me home, I was in no mood to talk to anyone. I locked myself inside my room and didn't step out for dinner also. I was feeling sickum-sick.

It was after eleven in thee night when my cell rang. It was Dingy calling. Before I could scream, 'Run Dingy run, run away and get married in Bangkok', she screamed. 'Thank you thank you thank you, Mahi! I told you, *na*….I told you, you could do it…I knew first itself that you could make Andeep's parents change their minds…all this is left hand's play for you…you've done bigger miracles…this is nothing…'

Hai, my bestie had gone mad with pain.

'Dingy, did you talk to Dumpy –?'

'Forget Dumpy! I spoke to Andeep. He said you did it. You made thee impossible possible…'

That *laudu*! He didn't have thee guts to tell her truth, so he was telling lies.

'Dingy, open your ears and listen to me…you don't know what happened…'

'I know everything, Mahi… But what I don't know is how you made them prepone thee wedding also…to November end…'

Hain?

The wedding had been preponed? To November end?

'I didn't even ask you to prepone it. But like my true best friend, you did it on your own. You knew I couldn't wait till Feb…You knew I couldn't live without Andeep for three long months…now I've to be away from him for only two weeks…'

My head started rotating. It was possible or what? Could Sutlej river flow backwards? Could Vikram Bhatt make hit movie? Could BJP and Congress join together into one party?

'They want to meet you again…discuss Bangkok in detail…Dumpy's free tomorrow… go and settle everything once and all, okay…please please please?'

I was too tired to do you-you-me-me (oho, argument) with her. I said okay, hanged up and fell asleep.

I woke up and patted thee side table for my cell. Ready to delete thee fifty-one Good Morning WhatsApps Bhooto sent every morning. I stared at thee screen in confusion. Something was wrong. Either my cell was dead or Bhooto was. Leave fifty-one, there was not one WhatsApp from her.

There was only one WhatsApp. From my old client Binu Gujral (she pronounced it 'Guzral'). She owed me – meaning, she owed Ludhiana to London – thirty grands for planning her granddaughter's birthday party. Said she wanted to make thee payment now means now. I was thinking how thee sun rose from the South when –

'*HAI!*' Came Bhooto's cry.

This time I didn't rush out of thee room. I stretched, yawned, put feet inside slippers with art movie speed. And then I walked out of thee room in slow motion.

Bhooto was sitting on thee dining table, head down. Like ghosts in horror movies, she suddenly sat up. Gave me one look and burst out crying.

What new *chutiyapa* now, I thought in irritation. Then suddenly, I was scared.

Was it Niku? Did he have accident? I started imagining all bad-bad things. Niku lying dead on thee road. Flies flying on his face. Dog doing *susu* on him.

'Mummyji! Where's Niku? Is he okay?'

'Niku's fine. He's still sleeping.'

I looked at thee clock. Strange, Niku was not late sleeper or late store-goer. 'He's not gone to thee store?'

'*Arre*, what will he do at thee store. No one's going to come today.'

'Why? Is it Bharat Bandh today?' I asked jokily.

Bhooto picked up remote and switched on TV.

"*…Bold move that takes the nation by surprise… PM demonetizes five hundred and thousand rupee notes…*" Thee TV anchor was yelling.

Then only it striked to me. So this was what Raj was talking about. This was thee appointment thee PM had with the whole nation.

Note-ban. *Note-bandi*. Demonization? The words kept eating circles my head.

Ya, it was shocking. But what for us? We were normal level people who acted like high level people. Earning hundred, spending thousand. This was rich people's problem. People who had suitcases of black money... people like... Binu Gujral! Oho, so that's why Madam was finally giving me my money...

Suddenly, I slapped my forehead. Then I understood! *That* was Andeep's Daddyji Mummyji's game! So that's why they wanted finger-click wedding.

They wanted to get rid of all their old black money! *Saale!*

I was angry with God and government and thee whole world. But then I thought, leave. Why to burn my blood? At least, my bestie's dream would come true.

'*Hai*, what will I do now?' Mummyji was slapping her chest and crying like anything. She hadn't cried like this even when Papaji had died.

'Mummyji, we don't have to do anything.'

'But all our savings...turned to dust.'

'Good, no, we don't have too many savings.'

Guilty look came on her face.

My eyes became big. 'You have savings?'

'Little bit,' Bhooto said, trying to get up from the dining table.

I stared at her so badly, she sat back on thee chair.

'How much?'

'Oh, I haven't counted.' She replied, but from her expression, I knew that she was lying.

'How much, Mummyji?'

'Six lakhs.'

My life went out. 'Six lakhs?' I repeated, not at all sure I'd heard right answer. 'You have six *lakh* rupees? At home? In your room? In that Godrej almirah?'

'And some under my mattress. And some inside my locker. And some in my safe…'

I *toh* couldn't bear to hear more. Last week, she'd been crying saying she had no savings. And now she was crying saying she didn't know what to do with her savings. I felt like one *chu@#$%*. She was faster than bullet train. She'd kept so much cash and not one '*chu*' had come out of her mouth.

'Why didn't you tell me, Mummyji?' Niku's voice came from behind.

She turned around and her face became white.

'Niku!' She gasped.

'When I was looking for loan? You knew I was asking people for money. But not once did you open your mouth and say…'

Hai, poor Niku had faced such tough times. If I had any money, I'd have given him happily. But my bank balance was so low, so low, it was lower than Bhooto. How could she stab her own son in thee backside? I *toh* couldn't believe.

Tears started running down her cheeks. 'I was keeping it as security for my old age…'

'Because I was going to throw you out? Put you in old-age home?'

'No, no…please, Niku…listen to me…'

But Niku was in no mood to listen. He walked out of the house, slamming the main door behind him.

Bhooto crumpled like old Delhi building on thee dining-table.

She wanted sympathy from me, but I didn't feel like giving it. What she'd done was wrong. Plus, there was no time. Dumpy was picking me up for long drive to Bathinda in one (if he was on time) or two (if he was late like last time) hours.

Thee whole environment had changed.

Uncleji Auntyji were standing outside thee house with full *tabbar* (oho, family). Andeep, his sister Gurdeep, her husband Amanjeet, their two childrens, Limca, senior citizen and two other staff members. Only things missing were *dhol-walas* and *phool-malas* (oho, drum-beaters and flower garlands).

'Come, *puttar ji*, come,' Uncleji said.

We touched knees (not our own, Uncleji's and Auntyji's), before following them inside.

'Hmm,' I began, taking my position next to thee tiger. 'So, Uncleji Auntyji, I hear you want thee wedding in Bangkok?'

'Bangkok and only Bangkok,' Uncleji said. Auntyji moved her head up and down so hard, I thought she'd get spondylitis.

'But it's thee question of your only son's wedding,' I said with fake concern.

'We've full confidence that only you will do great job.'

'But I don't have much experience.'

'How will young people get experience, *haan*? How? If we don't give them chance?'

'Daljit! Daljitey!' Auntyji called out.

Senior-Citizen came in carrying tray with two tall lassi glasses. But this time, I was fast. I made my fingers wiggly-wiggly, called him towards me and picked up both thee glasses.

'That was for –' Uncleji began.

I raised one eyebrow like Kathak dancer.

'You, it's for you,' Uncleji gulped. 'Have, have.'

I had. First thee first glass, then thee second glass. Taking loud sips.

'Can we say we're having destination wedding?' Auntyji started when I finished thee lassi. 'We're not less than anyone…'

They were not. They were the biggest *laudus* I'd seen.

'We're also modern-shodern, we can also move with thee times…'

'But how will we fly thousand-and-one guests for thee *baraat*?' I continued in voice cooler than thee lassi.

'It's not possible,' Uncleji told Auntyji firmly. 'We'll take only family – we two, Gurdeep-Amanjeet and theirs two. It's our son's wedding, not Kumbh Mela. Plus, Dingy's also bringing only family –'

'And me and Bhoo–means, my Mummyji and Niku,' I informed him, in case he was thinking of cutting our cards also.

'Of course, of course,' he agreed, 'you're family.'

'And one of my close friends,' Andeep put in quickly. 'He's also like family.'

'So guest matter's finished,' Uncleji said, raising his hands.

But I hadn't finished bajaoing their band. 'But you've eaten at so many weddings…'

'Mostly thee food was bad. Better not to call such people.'

'But what will you tell your friends?' I taunted Uncleji.

'Andeep says your brain runs faster than computer. You only suggest something, Mahi *Beta*.'

'Hmm,' I stroked thee tiger, thinking loud: 'Why don't we say that Andeep and Dingy…' I struggled to think of thee word for boy-girl running away to get married…what it was…enveloped? anteloped? Then I thought what difference, as if they were all Shakespeare's relatives sitting in front of me. 'Enveloped?'

'Enveloped?' Uncleji asked, scratching his beard.

'She means "eloped", Papaji. It means running away to get married,' came Andeep's voice.

I was so surprised (oho, not because he finally spoke up, because he knew that much English) I swallowed too much lassi and started coughing.

Uncleji's bum lifted and for one second, I got tension that he was going to rub my backside.

I put one hand up like referee. 'I, I'm,' I coughed, 'fine now.'

Uncleji's bum went down. So did my tension level.

'Yes, yes, elope. It means running away to get married.' I continued like knowledgeable person. 'But because you're big-hearted, you decided to forgive and went to Bangkok to give blessings.'

Uncleji Auntyji looked at each other.

'Worried about your social position?' I asked sweetly.

'Who cares about people…their job is to talk…but we've to think about our financial position, no?' Auntyji made face. 'Oho, what's there to think, just say okay.'

'Okay,' Uncleji said slowly. 'Andeep, go bring money.'

'Did I hear you correctly, Uncleji? You're going to pay for thee wedding?'

'Yes, *Beta*.'

'But you are boy's side,' I sunaoed them their own dialogue. 'How can you pay for thee wedding?'

'What boy side, girl side,' Uncleji said waving my 'protest' away. 'We are all one side, one family. We'll give fifty percent of wedding expenses. Andeep, get suitcase.'

Like trained dog, Andeep leaped from sofa and went running to get it.

'I was telling your Aunty last night only that this Mahi, very talented,' Uncleji started putting soap all over me. 'Too good she is.'

I showed my teeth to him. First time, he'd said something sensible.

Andeep came back carrying old brown suitcase and placed it next to me. I bent down to pat it, feeling like smuggler.

'We want their wedding in two weeks,' Auntyji added.

Kameene! They just wanted to get rid of their cash before thee demon...demonization...oho, note-ban deadline. What materialist, money-minded, monkeys Dingy was marrying.

I opened my mouth, but Dumpy gave me look.

'Uncleji Auntyji, you've come to thee right person. Let's do *balley-balley* in Bangkok.'

'I told you, no, this girl could do anything.' After putting soap on me, Uncleji gave me shower. Oho, with praises.

'So, it's settled then?' Dumpy asked.

Uncleji Auntyji nodded.

'Badhaiyaan!'

Everyone started saying 'Congrats congrats' to everyone.

'What's for lunch?' Uncleji asked Auntyji.

'Biryani, butter chicken, naan...'

My throat and stomach both made loud sounds.

'And sweet-dish?'

'Besan laddoos and rabdi…'

I was thinking I'd leave their house two kg heavier, when Uncleji got up and folded his hands.

'Okay, *ji*. See you in Bangkok.'

Everyone started saying 'Bye-bye' to everyone.

I *toh* couldn't believe they were such *kanjoos makhichoos* (oho, miser fly-suckers).

I gave Dingy congo (not country, congratulations) thee second we got into thee car.

'So along with wedding, you can have your spinster party in Bangkok…you'll be landing in Bangkok few days before thee wedding because you're…' I struggled to remember thee word.

'Eloping,' Dumpy provided it.

'I can't believe my dream's going to come true,' Dingy sighed after I'd finished telling her thee whole story. 'I'll wear my designer *lehenga*…

'Anmol Chaddha's not designer,' I interrupted. 'she's copycat. Local tailor who copies thee work of all famous designers…'

Dingy ignored and went on, '…And walk down thee beach –'

Hain? 'Beach?' I asked in hello-are-you-all-right voice. 'There's no beach in Bangkok.'

'WHAT?' Dingy cried out, sounding like dog from whom I'd snatched bone.

'No Beach Bangkok,' I repeated clearly just in case she'd not heard thee first time.

'B-b-but, but it's my dream to have beach wedding in Bangkok…' she cried. 'How will I get married without beach?'

First Bangkok. Then beach. Life was bitch.

I banged my head against my cell phone three times.

'Do something, Mahi-ve !' Dingy begged.

Arre, what could I do? From where I could give birth to beach in Bangkok?

'You've my swear, Mahi! Swear to God you'll see my dead face.'

If she gave swear for every *chintu* thing, forget me, even God wouldn't take her seriously. But then her CD (Crying Dying) started. And my heart became loose again.

'Dingy, please, control. I'll do something,' I said in rough voice.

And that's how I was stuck in Hua Hin.

Andeep's Delhi contact had made discovery of thee *piddu* island close to Bangkok. It was very short notice. And all thee hotels were fully booked after two weeks. Except one. Hotel Lembla.

7

In which the former groomie becomes current roomie

Tarzan came back to thee room, cutting my flashback. He looked like he'd scored centum in all subjects in thee Board Exams.

'Well, this is a surprise,' he spoke up. 'When I was booking the resort, they told me –'

'You booked thee resort?' I gasped.

'You're welcome,' he replied.

'But Andeep said…' Then only it strriked to me. 'You're Andeep's Delhi contact!'

He bowed down like magician after magic show.

I almost burst like pressure-cooker with too much steam. Andeep knew everything means EVERYTHING, but still he did this! I wanted to kill that *laudu*, but I didn't want to make Dingy widow before her marriage.

Tarzan had no idea of thee volcano bubbling inside me. 'As it happens, there's a room available –' he said excitedly.

My face became small. I thought he'd made evil plan to force me to share room. So when I saw him looking all happy to shift to separate rooms, I was irritated like anything.

'I'll take it,' I cut him.

'Hear me out, Mahender. I'm not done…'

'But I am,' I jumped down from thee bed and slipped my feets inside thee fluffy hotel slippers. 'I don't want to spend one minute extra in this room…I want thee other room right now –'

I wanted to show that I was more eager to shift out.

'Not room, suite. The honeymoon suite,' he finished thee sentence, meow type look coming on his face.

Haw!

I was shockum-shocked.

'I'm not exactly dying to get into a honeymoon suite either,' Tarzan said, seeing my expression.

Control, Mahi, control. He didn't say, 'I don't want get into honeymoon suite *with you*, Mahi'. He just said he didn't want to enter honeymoon suite. I knew he was anti-marriage from thee beginning. I knew all that, but still, I felt so hurted. I'd walked out of our flat in Delhi, but suddenly, I felt like thee rejected one.

I ignored thee chest pains on my right side. 'I don't mind getting into honeymoon suite,' I said sweetly. 'but not with you.'

That's it, his smile became *phurrrrr*.

Good, I thought with satisfaction. Let him also feel thee pinch.

For thee next few seconds, there was *maha* tension in the room.

'So I'll tell Agung we won't be taking it?' He finally broke thee silence. 'He was going to give this room to a solo guest and bump us up to the suite.'

Agung. So that was Chusli's real name. So tough to remember. Thai people like complicating life, I went grumble-grumble. Why couldn't they be like Punjabis? Our names were so simple. Sweety, Pinky, Whitey. Just think of your favourite colour – and *phatttt* – you can remember thee name.

'Tell Agung we can't,' I said firmly. 'What will people say?'

How only it would look? Two of us alone in thee honeymoon suite. Like newly-married couple. Like two bodies, one soul. Like...

My heart became like Golden Band. Oho, thee most popular wedding band in Ludhiana. My inside voice started screaming at thee top of my lungs.

'God, you're unbelievable!' Tarzan said, shaking his head. 'You're prepared to spend the rest of the week with me, in this poky room, on this bed. But you won't share the honeymoon suite! Why? Because of "what will people think"? Who are these fucking people? And why do you give a shit about them? You could share a large, airy room with a sitting area and a couch...a couch I'd be willing to sleep on, gentleman that I am, leaving the kingsize bed to you...'

Sitting area? Couch? On top of that, king's bed?

I gave him Why-didn't-you–tell-before look.

He gave me I-was-trying-to look.

'Look at us talking without talking,' Tarzan mentioned, his lips twisting to one side. 'Only couples do that, you know?'

'We're not couple. We're India and Pakistan, Karan Johar and Ram Gopal Varma, we're...'

'And here I thought we were ice-cream and chocolate,' he said in low voice. Wicked look came on his face and he maaroed eye at me. I gasped.

Kutta! Kameena!

When we were not India and Pakistan, when we were one country, we'd done ice-cream and chocolate stunt together.

Before I could have flashback about that night, Tarzan threw rude question at me.

'We don't got all day, Mahendar. Yes or no? In or out?'

Hai, I was in – what was that word – didi-ma? dilli-ma? I was stuckum-stuck. I didn't know what to do. I'd to make choice. Think about people and stay stuck in pigeon's hole? Or show middle finger to people and go for king's bed? Think, Mahi, think.

I made up my mind. 'How soon can we get thee honeymoon suite?'

Tarzan gave slow smile. 'I'll ask Agung to get on it right away.'

He left thee room and I sat down on the bed with loud *dhammm.*

Why you're tense, Mahi? my inside voice asked. *You've jumped into different bed with same boy.* Inside voice was right, but still. I also had some standard. I couldn't jump in and out of different beds with same boy.

Then I thought, by thee time wedding party came from Bathinda and Ludhiana, thee resort would be empty. We'd shift into separate rooms and no one would know thee truth.

It was just thee matter of seven days. It couldn't be that bad.

It was worst.

It was total *syapa*! No, it was *Syapa* with capital S. No, no, it was *SYAPA* with all capitals letters.

'I hope you'll like a labia,' Chusli said politely, inserting card into honeymoom suite.

Tarzan's eyes became wide in shock. 'I *beg* your pardon?'

Chusli pointed to thee board outside room, looking like calm monk.

'Arabian Nights,' Tarzan read thee theme aloud. 'Oh, you meant Arabia.'

'A labia, yes,' Chusli nodded. Tarzan burst out coughing again.

'Now if theme suspense is broken, can we go inside?' I said in bored tone.

Chusli held thee door open. I went in and my tongue came out.

The sitting area was SESKI! Means, hundred times more than sexy! Small settee, colourful cushions, thick carpet, scented candles, lamp shade. I looked at thee ceiling and saw stars. I looked at thee wall and saw camels – means, camels wallpaper. There was hookah next to thee settee.

'I *toh* love it,' I made declaration.

And like always, put both feets in my mouth.

Because when we followed Chusli inside, '*haw*' look came on my face. Thee bedroom was some *tharki* old sheikh's dirty fantasy come true. Red and pink decor. Round bed, heavy silk curtains hanging from it. Chusli pressed button. And it started rotating. Not my head, the bed.

Next to thee bed was small trolley with jugs and glasses on it. And bunch of black grapes. Hot scene came into my mind. Me in black harem pant and cut-off sleeve flowing pink top, balancing jug on my right shoulder, feeding Tarzan black grapes....

I looked up and saw him looking at me, wicked smile on his face. *Hai*, did he know I was dirty day dreaming? Thank god he couldn't see inside my head. I turned red like London bus and turned face away.

'And that's the walk-in bathloom,' Chusli said proudly. Like he'd made thee bathroom with his own hands.

We walked into thee bathroom straight. Because – *hayo rabba* – here no door! Only glass walls! It started rotating. Not thee bathroom, my head.

This time *toh*, I had to look at Tarzan. He'd big wolf's smile on his face, like he'd maaroed some big arrow.

Thee minute Chusli left, I turned to him.

'I want to change...'

'Go right ahead...I'll close my eyes,' he replied.

'Not my clothes. Thee room.'

'Why?'

Kutta!

He knew why. He just wanted to play cat-mouse game with me.

'I-I just don't like it.'

He dropped down on thee bed. 'Can't imagine why,' he said innocently, joining his hands under his head in relaxed pose. 'It's a perfectly nice room.'

'For Alibaba or Aladdin...' I said, ice in my voice.

Tarzan burst out laughing.

'And look at that toilet!' I cried out, pointing one hand at it. 'Hotel would have become bankrupt or what if they had put one bloody door?'

'Oh come on, Mahendar, don't be a prude.'

I crossed my arms over my boobies. 'Hello, if you think I'm going to go to thee bathroom in front of you...'

'Nothing I haven't seen before,' he said in pussycat type tone.

What cheeks!

I picked up thee pillow and threw it violently at him. He bent down so it went and hit thee Arabian jug. The jug started rocking left and right like it was drunk.

Tarzan held up his hands. 'Okay, okay, I completely agree that some things should be left to the imagination –'

'What for you? You're boy,' I almost spit thee words out.

'Hey, it may come as a complete surprise to you, but I don't want anyone to watch me do my business either.'

'Your business?' I repeated like dumb parrot, confused. 'What business are you going to do inside thee bathroom?'

'What guys do inside the washroom...'

He left thee sentence incomplete and gave me meaning-wallah look.

I desperately wanted to act cool-shool like him and throw his dialogue 'Nothing I haven't seen before' back on his face.

But I was Mahi, not Lavith. I marched out of thee room then and there. Marched straight to Reception counter.

Chusli gave me big smile. 'Miss Ahulwalia, how may I help you?'

Bas, I burst out. 'Only you can help me, Chu...I mean, Mr. Reception...I want to change thee room.

His smile vanished like it was *daag* (not dog, stain) and I was Surf Excel. 'Can...not.'

'Can can,' I insisted.

'Solly, all looms book.'

'I'll pay you.'

'No can.'

'Yes can,' I said desperately.

After few more minutes of can can and can...not, I accepted defeat. If I'd fought my tongue with Chusli for one more minute, I'd have gone mad.

'What happened,' Lavith asked innocently when I went back. 'Your magic didn't work?'

'Chusli not budging.'

'Chusli?' Tarzan smile was like Bhakra Nangal Dam, stretching from here to there.

I must have looked like suicide case, because he said with full sympathy, 'Look, it won't be so bad. Send me a text each time you go to the loo, just to be on the safe side. Okay?'

'But,' I hesitated, 'what if you have to...?'

He gave me encouraging look. 'I have to?'

'To do *susu* badly,' I said at last.

His corners – means, his mouth corners started moving. 'I won't,' he ate swear, serious expression on his face. 'Even if I need to do *susu* badly, I won't barge in. Bad though it is for my health, for my bladder, I'll hold it in. Gentleman's promise. Happy?'

Such big sacrifice. *Hai*, he *toh* was touching me so much. I gave tight smile like old person who had done too much Botox.

I breathed out, relived. But situation was still tensed. It was like Wagah border. Even when there's no war, small shootings take place every day. But no one minds. Everyone thinks it's normal.

I went out to the sitting area, and was about to drag my strolley to thee room.

'Allow me,' Lavith said and picked it up like it was feather.

Small blush came on my face. He used to pick me up also. Like I was feather. At thee memory, small tear came to my eyes. I swallowed it quickly, but Tarzan had seen my expression.

He again misunderstood. But thank god, he did. Because if he knew the real reason, I *toh* wouldn't be able to face him.

'Look, I know how you feel about us planning the wedding together…'

Planning? Wedding? Together? *Bas,* that was enough to change my mood. He was comparing himself to me? To Mahi, who had six-years experience and lifetime knowledge of planning events? *Saala!* Zero% experience, 100% overconfidence.

'You and plan wedding!' I went snort-snort like pig.

His lips became thinner than Anushka's lips before she put plumpy injection. 'If you're going to be like this…'

'No, no, sorry, please tell what you're thinking…'

'Okay,' he started. 'I was thinking why don't we split duties?'

Arre, it was wedding. Not some pizza or sweet-dish.

'I can't leave anything to chance,' I said slowly. Or to him. But that I didn't say loudly.

'But you're not. You're leaving it to me.'

'Same difference,' I said, lifting one shoulder.

His eyes became narrow. 'That's the problem with you. Once you take a stand, you simply won't give an inch.'

'I can't give inch, centimetre, kilometre. Oho, I can't! You don't understand…I can't! Dingy's my best friend – no, she's like my *sister*. It's my duty and responsibility and job to give her dream wedding. And I swear to God, even if I die, I will.'

'If you die, how will you be of any use to her?'

I continued like he hadn't said anything. '…I want everything – everything – to be first class, tip-top, A-One. If anything goes wrong…' I left sentence incomplete to shiver, 'never in thousand years will I be able to forgive myself…'

Soft look came into his eyes. And I came to sudden halt.

'What?' I asked him.

'It's sweet, the way you care for Dingy. But I wish you'd trust me. I won't let you down, you know. Ever.'

Breeze blew in from thee open window, making me go *brrrr*. He was still talking about thee wedding or?

I made thee mistake of looking into his brown eyes. And immediately, gooses (not birds, dots) came on my arms, legs and other areas. He reached for my hand.

ZOINGGG!

I felt as if he'd plugged it into electric socket. From zero battery, I suddenly became 100% charged. My heart started beating like out-of-control wild animal. My legs started going diggy-diggy. My mind started screaming *Bhaag Milkha Bhaag*. All this from touching his hand. Imagine what would have happened if he'd touched other, more important, body parts.

I pulled my hand away like he was microwave at three hundred degree temperature. That skull and bones sign on dangerous things should be put on Tarzan also, I thought, my heart racing like metro rail.

I had to put space between us. I walked to thee intercom to make call.

'Loom selvice,' came thee voice.

I put phone away from my mouth. 'I'm ordering loom, oho, room service. You want?'

He shook his head and walked out of thee bedroom. I collapsed on thee bed.

Hai, one day close to Tarzan was torture of thee first order. How only I was going to manage seven?

8

In which swords are cross and heated words are exchanged

'Sir, Madame? Good molning. I'm Paul, your Wedding Advisol,' thee man at thee reception greeted us. Immediately, I named him Muesli, because he looked like Chusli's healthy version.

'It's not our wedding,' I said without thinking.

'No, it's not,' Tarzan said with straight face. But I could see that he was dying to laugh.

It was not my fault. My mind was not working only. I got sleep disturbance thee night before. Oho, not because thee Arabian bed was uncomfortable, because I was uncomfortable. Tarzan was so close to me. Just outside thee bedroom door. Rolling on thee settee. Wearing tight-shite whitey-lightey *chaddi*. Or maybe not even that…

'Lavith,' Tarzan said, putting his hand out.

Muesli took it so lovingly, for one second I was worried he'd kiss it.

When he didn't, I safely gave my hand to Muesli. 'Myself, Mahi. Top Wedding Planner from Ludhiana.'

'Nice to be part of your wedding, Madame, Sir.'

'It's not our wedding,' Lavith said, his eyes doing bhangra.

Saala!

He was having good time at my expense. And he didn't even have decency to cover up. He was wearing his holiday uniform. Flowery short shorts and deep V neck tee shirt. His naked chest was giving sneak peeks and calling me...

I used my yoga powers to look at thee other man in uniform. 'Mr. Mues –'

'Paul, his name is Paul,' Tarzan supplied.

'Mr. Paul, can you suggest good venue for wedding?'

'Lembla is the best venue for wedding.'

Uff!

'I mean inside Lembla Resort.'

His light bulb was switched on. 'Ah! If you'll follow me?'

'Surely we will,' I said.

And we did. All thee way to thee manicured-pedicured lawn side-by-side to thee sea.

'You can have lawn wedding,' Muesli said, spreading his arms widely.

Sprinklers were on. They were watering thee grass and giving me thee *susu* feeling. But it was good idea.

'We can put thee *mandap* here, sea facing,' I said, excited.

'Then the audience's back would be to the sea. How about we place it there?' Tarzan pointed opposite side. 'Also sea facing, but for the guests. In any case, Andeep and Dingy will have eyes only for each other.'

I peesoed my teeths. I knew what Tarzan was doing. He was cutting my suggestion knowingly. With lot of difficulty, I kept my temperature and voice down.

'We can put bar here,' I said, going up to thee coconut tree. 'Bartender can pour vodka into thee coconuts right in front of their eyes –'

'What about the guests who don't have vodka?'

Limited guests were coming. And I'd made list of who drank what.

'Everyone drinks vodka,' I said like one proudy.

'I don't.'

'I know,' I said with my nose in thee air. 'Too much heat in your body.'

I regretted after speaking. I knew he got pimples after drinking vodka. It was better to avoid all personal topics. But like person wearing white clothes has to, has to go in puddle and become dirty, I did too.

Tarzan raised an eyebrow. 'Heat in my body?'

Ya, when you drink vodk –' I saw his cheap expression and changed thee topic immediately. 'You can have whiskey. Your body won't be hot then.'

'No? Sure about that?'

Hai, I thought, not even looking, his shoulders and chest and what not. He'd always be *totta* (not parrot, hot boy). I turned red like post-box.

'Okay, but what about food?' I changed topic like bad driver who suddenly changes lanes.

'When would you like to taste us?' Muesli asked politely.

'Never, I hope,' Tarzan replied, rolling his eyes towards thee sky.

'We're very eager for you to taste us,' Muesli insisted.

'Mr. Mue, I mean, Mr –'

Tarzan gave me 'You forgot his name again' look.

'Please call me Paul,' Muesli told me politely.

Arre, I was going to call him Paul. That was his name, no?

'Can you give me your special menu? I'll see what works.'

'*We'll* see,' Tarzan corrected me. 'We'll see what works.'

I made face as if I'd swallowed big tablet (not Samsung, medicine) and continued talking. 'Mr. Mues...I mean, Mr,' I struggled to remember his name but failed. 'I know you cannot offer Indian cuisine, but what else can you offer apart from Thai? Chinese? Italian?'

'Lembla's Chinese chef lan away.'

I slapped my forehead inside me head. *Phitte muh!* His chef had to run away now only.

'Okay... what about Italian?'

'Chinese chef lan away with Italian chef.'

I slapped my forehead actually this time.We were stuck with only Thai food. It was problem, big problem. Andeep's Jungle Brigade had to be fed Indian or they would go wild.

'Your website said international cuisine,' I accused Muesli. 'Or did your website designer lun away too?'

I was justified angry. It was thee heights. Writing lies on website. Taking inno-cent customers for rides. I wanted to open Trip Advisor and give them zero-star review.

I gave Tarzan, 'Now please don't say everyone lies on website' look.

He gave me, 'Don't worry, we'll manage' look.

'One second, Paul, we'll just have a quick word. Mahi?'

We stepped away from Muesli to have personal talks.

'Okay, you know what, why don't we call someone from Ludhiana?' Tarzan suggested.

'And who'll finance that, Arun Jaitley?' I growled. 'My budget's limited.' Uncleji had given me only one suitcase of cash, but it wasn't fully packed like they show in movies.

'Mine's not,' he said with shrug. 'I don't mind paying from my own pocket.'

'Next, Muesli will say there's no photographer, then? What-what will you pay for?'

'A wise person once told me, "Food's the most important thing at a wedding", and…'

I stared at him, shocked. Wise person hadn't told him that. I had.

'…so, whatever it takes…' Tarzan continued. 'You're not the only one who wants the wedding to be a super-duper hit, you know…'

My mind wheel had stopped turning only. He remembered my dialogue. Dialogue that I'd said many months back. Flashback came flashing to my head. And my mind went flying back to that day.

It was late in thee night. We were in his flat. Tarzan had just come back from work.

I was sitting on thee sofa, box of vanilla ice-cream with chocolate syrup in my hand, watching TV. He came and sat down next to me.

'Sorry I'm late,' he said, rolling up his sleeves.

Even thee sight of his muscles-shuscles didn't cool me down. I was irritated means irritated. Every night was late night. Every night it was same story. Every night he said sorry.

I stayed quiet like kneaded dough.

'What you thinking, baby?'

'I'm thinking that you're thee night-watchman of your bank.'

'I'm thinking someone's pissed off,' he said, giving me melty smile.

'Right answer,' I said, acting like reality show judge and giving him three slow claps.

'Are you going to ask me if I've eaten?'

'Are you going to ask me to cook if you've not?' I asked.

My shoe only I was going to cook in thee middle of thee night. I'd not cooked for myself also. After thee client meeting at Rajouri Gardens, I'd finished two plates of momos.

'Wouldn't dream of it,' Lavith replied. 'If you want to eat at twelve in thee night, call restaurant, not me.' Don't worry, I know your instructions by heart.'

'Good.' I turned my attention back to TV.

'What I don't know is what you told Mrs Kothari,' he said casually adjusting his sleeves.

I'd given that useless Mrs Kothari good in thee evening. I knew thee news would reach Tarzan, but I didn't know it would reach so soon.

'That she's *chutiya* of thee first order,' I replied in calm voice, without removing my eyes away from TV screen.

'Hmm,' he said, placing his legs on thee centre table. I snatched thee remote which was lying in thee middle of us. 'Dare I ask why?'

'Because food's thee most important thing about thee wedding.'

'I thought the couple's the most important thing about the wedding. But perhaps I'm wrong.'

'You're wrong.'

'Well, you're the expert,' he agreed.

'I am. And when I say Minakshi Kothari's butter chicken is rubber chicken, you better believe.'

He reached for my hands. I didn't pull them away. 'I do believe you, Mahi, but I don't understand –

'What don't you understand?' I cut him. 'People come to weddings to eat...also to get jealous and to pass bitchy comments...but most importantly to eat. And I don't want my reputation as wedding-planner to go down because thee food is shit.'

'Wedding planner?' he teased. 'I thought you were going to be a party-planner and nothing else but a party planner.'

It was true. I planned weddings only as exception. But Neeru Aunty, Tarzan's mother had asked me to organize her close friend's daughter's wedding. And I was trying my best to do it.

'At thee ladies sangeet, thee food was yucks. I didn't want flop show at thee wedding also.'

'I get it, totally understand,' he nodded. 'Am not saying you're wrong. But did it have to come down to this? Fighting and name calling? Couldn't you have talked things over, you know, in a more civilized fashion?'

I was really bugged up. I didn't know why Tarzan was acting like bapu (not my father, Father of thee Nation).

I snatched my hands away. 'Oh, ya? And what happened last week. When thee traffic signal near your office stopped working and there was big jam and you got stuckum-stuck? You acted in civilized fashion?'

'That's different. I was venting because nothing works in this damn country, nothing.'

'Hello, you're also part of this country,' I said crossing my arms over my chest.

'For now,' he said it voice lighter than idli.

I became stiffer than cardboard. It was touching topic for me. Tarzan never wanted to live in India. Never wanted to live in. Never wanted to get married. Because he was real life bastard. Father made mother pregnant. They didn't marry. After many years, when she asked him to accept them, he refused. Made her do DNA test. Finally, they got married last year. When their child was of marriageable age.

Many other things had happened last year. Oho, I'd saved Tarzan's life. We'd said love you love you to each other. He'd said bye-bye to New York and moved to Delhi. I'd said bye bye to Ludhiana and moved into his flat in Delhi.

But I couldn't stop thinking that he'd go back to thee States. That he was in India only because he felt guilty. That he was living in with me only because I'd saved his life.

My heart and face both shrank like clothes, like badly dry-cleaned clothes. But thanks to God Tarzan didn't notice. His eyes were on thee TV.

'What's that crap you're watching on TV?'

'Better than thee crap you keep watching on your laptop, Lav,' I replied sweetly.`

He turned to give him unbelieving look. 'You're calling *Game of Thrones* crap?'

'You're calling *Sasural Simar Ka* crap?'

'Doesn't it have that same mother-in-law-daughter in-law nonsense?' He went snort-snort.

I also gave loud artificial laugh. 'As if your *Game of Thrones* is any different. What was that *chudail* mother-in-law in it doing? Making her daughter-in-law walk *nangu pangu* in thee whole city.'

'Cersei and Marjorie!' Tarzan chuckled. 'Touche. I didn't know you were paying attention, baby.'

'*Arre*, it was on full blast on thee laptop, how could I not pay attention?'

'Right now, I can pay attention only to one thing,' he said, rubbing his nose on my neck.

My heart started banging my chest. I knew what he meant from my experience.

'The ice-cream.'

'Oh,' I said, offering thee bowl to him. 'Here, have.'

Tarzan shook his head. 'Not like this.'

He dipped his finger in thee bowl, brought some out and spread it on my neck. Then he leaned forward and slowly started licking it...

I was still tasting him – mean, tasting thee ice-cream when Tarzan clicked his fingers and forced me to come back to thee present. To Hawa-Hawai island. My yummy flashback melted then and there.

'Mahi? Mahi? You there?' he asked.

I came out of my coma. 'Ya – yes, I-I'm here only. Where else will I be?'

'So what do you think?'

'I can't think,' I said, pressing one side of my head. 'My head's blank.'

'No way! Your head's always buzzing with ideas and thoughts and possibilities.'

It was true. My brains were like our Prime Minister. Very active and always on thee move. My heart became softer than Sagar Ratna idli. I was touchum-touched at thee compliment.

'So, are you okay about flying the caterer out from Delhi?'

'But where he'll put up,' I asked. 'There are only eleven rooms in thee resort and –'

'We'll figure it out, okay?'

I was not at all sure, but what could I say except, 'Okay'.

Tarzan looked so relieved as if he had full glass Eno after wedding food. 'Great, so we can cross out catering from the to-do list. What's next?'

'Photo-grapher,' I informed. 'Please tell me you're not planning to offer thee job to Horsey.'

Last year in Goa, he'd called photo-grapher friend of his. She'd long face like horse, but used candid (not powder, shots) nicely. I didn't want to call her. Not last year, not now also. Oho, not because she was always touching and feeling Tarzan.

'I'm not. After the hard time you gave her, I'm sure she'd shoot the offer down.'

I made a face. 'I just wanted her to do her job. But she was interested in other jobs.'

Tarzan shook his head, his lips twisting.

'What?' I asked, my eyes challenging him to say what he was thinking.

He turned down thee challenge and turned to look at Muesli. 'Your website said something about an in-house photographer.'

Muesli moved his head like he was bobble doll. 'We're using the services of a freelancer, very good one.'

'Freelancer?' I asked. 'What's his full-time job?'

'Funeral photography.'

I burst out coughing.

'She nearly died at that,' Tarzan maaroed joke.

'Can we please have other option?' I begged desperately.

'Option?' Museli asked like he just couldn't understand why on earth I wanted option when death photographer was already there.

I expected at least Tarzan to understand that people were starting new lives, it would be unlucky, but even he joined Muesli. 'Why do you need an option?'

'I don't want someone who clicks dead bodies,' I hissed softly.

'Why not?' Tarzan argued. 'After all, marriage *is* the death of singledom. And think about the experience the funeral photographer will have clicking close ups,' Tarzan chuckled at his own joke.

'Funny joke.'

'I'm not being funny. For all you know, he'll have deadly photography skills…'

I didn't want to hear another death joke. 'Stop it, Lavith!' I hissed, covering my ears.

'We can't fly everyone down to Bangkok, Mahi.'

'So you'll decide whom we should fly and whom not?' I challenged him.

'Do you see anyone else around here?' he asked rudely.

'Ya, me,' I growled. Then I turned around and started walking away.

In two long steps, Tarzan reached me and grabbed my wrist. 'We're in this together, okay? Together. You can't just walk out of things, each time you don't like what's going on.'

9

In which dying embers are stoked and old fires are relit

I looked into his eyes. There were like Ajay Devgn's. Black, instense, burning with anger. I knew that he wasn't talking about thee wedding.

I shook my hand free and ran away. I went straight to our room – means, to thee room and locked thee door.

I picked up thee cell. There were ten WhatsApps from Raj. He still wanted job from me very badly. I didn't know how to make him understand. There was no place for him in my life – means, in Ludhiana to London.

I sighed and called Niku. The phone rang and rang, there was no reply. I called Bhooto, no reply. I called Dingy, no reply. I called Dumpy, no reply. Everyone who had place in my life was too busy to talk to me.

I sat like prisoner in thee room. I was so bored that I could only eat or sleep. I did both. First, I opened mini bar and ate all the chips and peanuts and chocolates. Second, I jumped on thee bed and straightened my back.

When I woke up, I decided to go for relaxing walk around thee resort. The walk was relaxing, till I saw Tarzan coming out of thee spa. He was wearing bath gown and towel-type slippers. *Bas*, I felt volcano of anger erupt from my body.

He was enjoying his international holiday, while I was *sadoing* (oho, rotting) alone in thee room.

Bas, then and there I decided that enough was enough. I wasn't going to spend more time thinking of thee past or thee future. I was going to live in thee moment. Only problem was, I didn't know how to. Either I was busy feeling guilty about thee past or feeling tensed about the future.

'Someone appears to be in a foul mood,' Tarzan commented.

'If I'd spent whole afternoon in spa, my mood would be good too,' I replied sweetly.

'So why didn't you?' he asked. 'You know, you deprive yourself too much.'

'You know, you pamper yourself too much. Too much money, have to spend on something, no?'

His lips pressed together and became *papad* thin. *Hai*, I *toh* wanted to bit my tongue for saying that. It was not his fault that he was rich. Okay, it was little bit his fault that he was rich. He did have family money, but he'd also worked for many years in thee States and earned in dollars-shollars.

'I don't know why I said that,' I said, biting my lip.

'I know. Because taunting me seems to be your favourite sport. It comes to your naturally. And if it were an Olympic event, you'd win gold –'

'I'm sorry, Lavith,' I said in small voice.

'It's okay, Mahi, I'm used to it,' he replied.

Hai, was I really giving him solid all thee time?

'Bye,' I said feeling little guilty.

I spinned around to walk away, but banged my toe hard against thee rocky landscape outside thee spa.

'OWWWWWWW!' I cried, painfully hopping on thee injured foot, trying to rub it at same time. I cursed myself for wearing rubber slippers and not my usual juttis with my Patiala salwar and short kameez.

'Sit,' Tarzan barked.

'Where? Here?'

'No, on the moon. Where do you think? On that rock. NOW!'

Tarzan gave command like circus ringmaster. I obeyed like trained lioness.

I sat on thee rock. He sat down on thee grass.

'May I? He asked.

I nodded, my heart racing faster than all thee Ferraris, Mercedes, BMWs in Ludhiana.

With gentle fingers, he took my foot out of my jutti and put it on his thigh.

SSSSSSSSSSSSIZZZZ!

Our bodies didn't contact each other directly – we were wearing clothes – but my skin started burning like I was walking on top of hot burning coals. I looked down. Straight into his eyes. They were like hot coals, too. But his hands, they were like cool water (not perfume, liquid).

Slowly, softly, expertly, he massaged my legs.

'You went to thee spa to get massaged or to learn how to massage?' I said jokily, because thee silence was killing.

'Shut up, Mahendar,' Tarzan whispered, 'Just shut up and relax.'

So I did. I closed my eyes and leaned back and let his fingers do thee magic.

'Stars up, handsome man down on you. Nice,' familiar voice broke into thee moment.

Tarzan dropped my foot like it was on fire. I opened my eyes to see Muesli smiling down at us.

'Jeez,' Tarzan muttered, 'your Muesli says the darndest things.'

'He's not my Muesli,' I protested, my voice rough.

'Madame? Sir?' Muesli leaned forward, trying to hear what we were saying.

'Nothing, nothing,' I said in hurry-burry, sitting up straight.

'Madame, Sir. If you'll follow me, 'I'll show you the album for the flower arrangements?'

I turned my nose up. 'Hello, Mister Mues –'

'Paul,' Tarzan supplied.

'Mr. Paul, I'm not going to use any ghisa-pita –'

Museli looked confused.

'Stale type idea,' I explained, 'for thee flower arrangement. It's my BFF's wedding, after all. I already have brilliant idea –'

'Then I'm sure you wouldn't mind going through the album,' Tarzan interrupted smoothly. 'Unless you're worried that your idea might suddenly pale in comparison?'

'Worried? Me?' I said like one proudy.

'I thought as much,' Tarzan said, pointing hand in thee direction of reception. 'After you, Paul.'

I put hand on my thigh and made effort to get up.

Tarzan and Muesli both offered me their hands. But I made wise decision and took Muesli's. Tarzan's eyes flashed angrily. He was acting as if I'd accepted Muesli's hand in marriage. How could I explain that I wasn't insulting him, I was just protecting myself. Touching Tarzan was like opening hot oven without gloves. And no Burnol, Boroline, Boro Plus could soothe that burn.

I limped to thee Reception, my feet and heart both heavy.

By thee time we finished going through thee bore flower arrangement album, it was dark.

'Dinner time,' I announced.

Tarzan's eyebrows went up. 'In some part of the world, yes.'

'In my part of thee world.' I had to, throw something down in my stomach.

'Dinner this early? Since when?'

'Since I left Del–,' I became red, 'since some time,' I changed my statement.

'Madame, Sir, would you like to have a plivate meal at our Livelside Velandah?'

'Private meal at Riverside Verandah?' Tarzan asked me.

'I'll *toh* eat anything, anywhere,' I declared, patting my growling stomach.

'Very good, Madame. This way, please.'

We followed Muesli again, this time to thee Riverside Verandah.

'I'll take your leave, Sir, Madame,' he said as we on sat down on thee cushioned bamboo chairs. 'Please don't forget to taste our bleasts…'

'Bleasts?' I was fully confused. 'Oh, you mean breasts.'

Muesli nodded. 'Our bleasts vely juicy…'

'*Arre*, when there are so many good good things on the menu, why we'll taste your breasts,' I said jokily.

'Hashtag facepalm,' Tarzan muttered.

Muesli bent down politely. 'Sir, Madame, I'll leave you then. Till tomollow. Have fun togethel at night.'

My cheeks became pinky-pink. I quickly put my face inside thee menu before Tarzan could see it. By thee time Mr. Waiter came, I was ready with my order.

'Stir-fried vegetable with soy sauce for me.' I leaned back against thee cushion and sighed as fresh river breeze tickled my face.

'I'll have the minced chicken and prawn with the peanut dip. You'll have the chicken satay, right?' He raised his eyes to look at me.

I nodded.

'Please get some extra chilli sauce for Madam,' he added.

Hai, he *toh* knew everything about me. Not everything, I reminded myself.

'Something to drink, Sir, Madam?' The waiter asked picking up thee beverage menu.

'I'm off drinks-shinks,' I said without thinking.

Tarzan's eyebrows went flying up as if Virat Kohli had retired from cricket.

'Only for some time,' I explained in hurry-burry, feeling little foolish. 'But you don't stop yourself.'

'Nah, I'm good. That will be all,' he dismissed thee waiter.

'Order what you want, *yaar*,' I insisted.

His lips stretched in big smile.

'I can't order what I want.'

'What?' I asked, confused.

'It's not on the menu,' he said in soft voice, strange look on his face.

I kept one minute silence like I was mourning our deadum-dead relationship.

'Were my ears playing tricks on me,' he spoke up, 'or did you just call me "*yaar*"?

'Your ears were not tricking you.'

'Hmm.' He leaned back in his chair. 'Does this mean we're friends, Mahendar?'

I raised one shoulder. 'I've been friendly only, Tarzan. You're thee one giving attitude.' I copied how he'd looked at me few minutes back. Made my lips thin, eyes narrow.

Tarzan's lips didn't stretch this time.

'With good reason. I'm the jilted party, remember? The rejected one. The dumpee.'

I was spreading napkin on my lap, but my hand stopped. Forget hand, my breathing stopped. My heart came leaping up to my throat.

'I-I didn't dump you,' I muttered. I pushed my chair back and got to my feet. In four five steps, I reached thee verandah's edge. I spotted one small sail boat in thee river and sighed. Because I felt like boat without sails.

He got up too and followed me. I looked up at him and my breathing stopped.

'You ran out on me, Mahi,' Tarzan growled like angry dragon.

'I didn't run out –'

'You left our place when I was abroad and didn't come back.' He spat thee words at me, his eyes shooting fireballs.

I joined my hands and started twisting them. 'I'd told you...on thee phone...that I...that I was going to leave.' I looked up into his eyes and my heart also twisted.

'That's not how I remember it. You said it wasn't going to work, I said we'd talk it over. I asked you to wait for me to come back, you agreed to wait. But you didn't, did you?'

'And I was right, don't you see now?' I cried out. 'How badly matched we were? Like keds with saree. Like tomato sauce with ice-cream. Like curd with noodles. It's all for thee best.'

'Is it, Mahi?' He narrowed his eyes, just like thee way I had when I was copying him.

Oh, what answer could I give to that?

'Aren't you happy?' I asked, turning my back to him.

He put his hands on my shoulders and turned me around. 'Are you?' He asked, his eyes searching mine for truth. But I couldn't tell him truth, I just couldn't.

'Yes, very,' I lied like expert, looking straight into his eyes. 'My work, you can see it's great, Niku's happy and Bhooto's – same old Bhooto... some things are like politicians, they cannot change... but, leave all that... I'm sure you're happy too...you've quit your job... how much you hated it! I-I'm sure you're enjoying life, meeting your parents...by thee way, how are are Dhiren Uncle and Neeru Aunty –'

'They are fine,' Tarzan cut me impatiently. 'But I don't want to talk about my parents. I want to talk about us –'

'There's no us,' I cried out, bringing my twisted hands up on his chest to push him away.

He caught them and pulled me to his chest. 'That's what I want to find out. Why? Why, Mahi? We were good together. We were happy. Sure, we'd our share of disagreements –'

'Fights,' I said sadly. 'Longer than Mahabharat, bigger than Panipat fights.'

'Nothing we couldn't get past,' he said firmly. 'We were working through the issues. Remember your "Make up before wake up" rule?'

How could I remember when I hadn't forgotten it only?

'So, what happened, Mahi. What got into you suddenly?'

'Nothing, nothing happened.' My voice was shaking.

'Don't you owe me an explanation? Don't I deserve that much?'

I shut my eyes tightly.

He deserved more. So did I. But I couldn't tell him that. I couldn't tell him anything.

Before I could control myself, one tear started running down my cheek. He bent down and kissed it. Before I could control him, he kissed me on my mouth. *Bas*, I went out of control. I started kissing him. And we kept kissing and kissing and kissing like someone had applied Fevicol to our mouths and then stitched them together.

It was Tarzan who unstitched them. Then only I realized what I'd done. I stepped back, looking and feeling guilty.

I'd told my heart so many times, 'Tarzan was bad for health, Tarzan was bad for health' but *kambakht* heart didn't understand. It didn't want to understand. Each time Tarzan came close, it started doing same cheater-type things.

I was so busy in my thoughts that I didn't notice Deepika, Anushka and two old men with musical instruments walk into the verandah. Tarzan's backside was to them. So he also didn't notice them.

He was going to say something, when suddenly dancing and singing started.

'What the fuck!' he hissed, spinning around.

Thee entertainment committee didn't bother to stop and continued their performance.

'For the love of God,' Tarzan said through peesoed teeth, 'Could we please have some privacy?'

'No!' I cried out, jumping between him and thee performers. 'I love singing and dancing.' My toe was paining badly, but my chest was paining more. And no Eno, Digene, Pudin Hara could make it go away.

Crazy look came into his eyes, like he wanted to murder all of us and go to jail.

Without thinking, I started copying whatever thee hell Anushka and Deepika were doing in thee name of dancing. They looked like delicate darlings doing graceful steps, but I looked like drunken monkey doing thee Lungi Dance.

10

The one with the impressive acting chops

I *toh* don't know how I sat through thee dinner. Forget thee vegetables I'd ordered, I felt stirred and fried by Tarzan's burning looks.

Anushka and Deepika left after one dance number, but thee singers kept us company throughout.

After thee main course, Tarzan ordered sweet-dish and coffee also. But thanks to his GO DIE looks, thee coconut milk and sticky rice felt like poison on my tongue. I made headache excuse and left thee table before thee waiter could bring coffee.

I went straight to our room – means, thee room and locked thee main door. I was sure Tarzan would follow me. I was more worried about what would follow after that.

I was right. Five minutes later, he was at thee door.

KNOCK! KNOCK!

'Mahi? Open the door,' Tarzan gave order.

This time, I didn't obey.

KNOCK! KNOCK!

'I know you're in there.

I kept shut up.

KNOCK! KNOCK!

'You know we need to talk.'

'No!' I cried out at last. 'There's nothing to talk.'

'I'm not leaving till you listen to me.'

'Then keep waiting.'

I kicked my slippers and marched into thee sheikh's sleeping chamber and threw myself on thee bed.

KNOCK! KNOCK!

I tried to ignore him and thee banging.

But this time, he didn't stop.

KNOCK! KNOCK!

After few seconds, I was sure all thee guests at Lembla would come running to our door.

I pulled myself up and marched towards the door, my temperature shooting up. 'Why don't you understand I don't want to kiss you –' I shouted as I pulled thee door open.

And died.

It was not Tarzan. It was Raj.

And he was looking at me like I was suicide bomber.

'I don't want to kiss you,' he gulped.

Uff!

I grabbed his hand and pulled him inside thee room.

'What are you doing here?'

'Requesting your permission to assist you for Dingy's wedding…'

I gave him 'what-are-you-talking' look. 'Dingy's wedding? That's in February. I'm here to plan –'

'Dumpy told me everything, Mahi.'

Phitte muh!

'Wait till I see that senseless Dumpy, one kick I'll give him. No sense he has. Acting like bloody Akashvani, announcing family secrets. No sense the bloody fellow has –'

'Please don't be angry with him, Mahi,' Raj pleaded. 'It's not his fault. He wasn't going to open his mouth, but seeing my condition –'

'You tried to commit suicide?' I gasped.

'Not yet.'

Not yet!

Hai, I *toh* got tense. What if he suicided and named me in thee letter? Police would put me behind thee bars. I loved bars but only thee ones that served whiskey vodka rum.

Uff! There were thousands of jobs, I don't know why he was after this. There were thousands of party-planners, I don't know why he was after me. I wanted to roll up thee carpet and hit him on thee head. But seeing his mental state, I didn't want to take unnecessary risk.

'Who else in Ludhiana knows that I'm in Bangkok, Raj?'

'Only me, God promise. You can trust me. With information and job both.'

'*Yaar*, I told you –'

'Please don't tell me no,' he begged. 'If you're worried about my salary, don't worry. I don't want money, I just want experience from you. Just try me for the position...'

'Shhh,' I whispered, worried about Tarzan. What if he'd come back and was standing outside and heard Raj? Surely he'd misunderstand...

Idea bulb got switched on in my head! It was better that Tarzan misunderstood! Maybe then he'd leave me and thee past alone.

'Mahi, I'm here in strict professional capacity,' Raj said in sincere voice. 'I want to be your assistant, nothing more, nothing less. Please don't think that – that I've dirty thoughts or cheap intentions about you.'

It was true, Raj had those feelings only for beer.

'You're much much older than me,' he added.

Hai, first his sister and now him. Both making me senior citizen.

I did 'Sit sit' action with my hand. He sat down on thee settee.

'Hmm,' I said, looking at him thoughtfully, plan forming in my mind at bullet-train speed. 'So you want to work with me with very badly?'

He moved his head up and down eagerly.

'How badly? Means, how far will you go to work with me?'

His eyes grew big.

'Means, what are you willing to do for me?' I sat down next to him and looked him straight in thee eye.

He jumped up in horror as if *I* had dirty thoughts and cheap intentions about him.

'I'm not willing to do THAT with you!' He put hand to cover thee round neck of his tee shirt as if I'd put hand on his honour.

'Yucks! I'm not asking you to!'

'Oh, thank god!' he said. He sat down again, joined both hands and looked at thee ceiling.

Hai, he *toh* was acting as if doing THAT with me was worst thing in thee world.

'I can do THAT with anyone I want,' I said proudly.

'But not with me, *na*?' he asked, worried look coming back in his eyes.

'Oye, calm down. You're not some Ranvir-Ranbir.'

I was also not some Katrina-Kareena, but at least one boy in Lembla wanted to do THAT with me. Thee thought made me both happy and sad at thee same time.

'So, what do you want from me?' Raj asked carefully, like any moment I'd try stunt with him.

'I want you to be my boyfriend.'

'WHAT?'

He jumped up again.

'Not real BF, just acting till we're in Bangkok.' I pulled him down.

'Oh, acting,' he repeated, relieved.

'Only acting,' I gave him my tongue. 'God promise I won't touch you...you'll be pure like lotus.'

'So, no hanky-panky?' Raj double-checked, taking out hanky from his pocket and wiping his sweating face.

'No touching-vouching, promise. Just once or twice, you'll have to do this.' I put both my hands around his neck and looked deep into eyes.

Poor thing got so nervous, he dropped thee hanky he was holding in his hand. I bent down to pick it up. And that's how Tarzan found us. Raj on thee settee, my head down between his knees.

'WHAT THE FUCK?'

I turned my head so suddenly, I almost got neck sprain.

The door! I'd left it open! Tarzan was standing there, looking like Yamraj (Oho, God of death).

Raj jumped up from thee bed, looking guilty like anything. I don't know why he was acting as if he'd been caught red-handed doing hanky-shanky.

I got into thee act immediately. 'Lavith,' I greeted him in cool voice, getting to my feet. 'Raj, meet Lavith, boy's side wedding-planner. Lavith, meet Raj, my BF –'

Tarzan's lips twisted. 'BF? As in Best Friend? Do people still say BF?

'BF as in boyfriend,' I interrupted smoothly. 'I don't know about people, but we still say BF-GF.' I turned to face Raj. 'Don't mind him, Raj, he's not our age. He's THIRTY.' I said it like it was dirty word.

Raj reached out to hold my hand like understanding BF. I *toh* was surprised. Oho, not because he caught my hand, because I didn't know he could act better than most of our Bollywood heroes.

Air-conditioning in room was on, but I started sweating. Would Tarzan believe my story? Would he stop coming behind me? Would he leave thee past alone? Would he stop asking questions?

Tarzan did ask question, but unexpected one. 'Are you trying to say that you both are the same age?'

Hai, thee day only was bad. Everyone was insulting me.

'Don't bother to answer, Raj. It's retory…restorical…'

'Rhetorical question,' Tarzan supplied. 'So, how long have you guys been, you know, a happy couple?'

'Last year –' I said.

'Last month –' Raj said at thee same time.

'Let me know when you agree on the timeline,' Tarzan said sweetly.

'We were casually dating-shating last year…before Goa,' I added, 'but became couple only last month…' I made up story quickly.

'I didn't know 'you had a boyfr – sorry, BF – last year.'

'There are lots of things you don't know about me,' I gave Tarzan taste of his own Crocin. 'Now what will you take to fuck off? And this isn't rhetorical question. We're meeting after many days, we need privacy.'

Tarzan took few long steps, but not towards thee door. He came and sat down – on thee settee.

'You need privacy, *you* fuck off. I ain't going nowhere,' he said leaning back against thee thick round pillows, which always reminded me of ding-dongs.

Uff!

He was like big stubborn horse. I wanted to give him same treatment that such horses are given. Kick him hard.

'Come, Mahi,' Raj said, bravely putting his arm around my waist. 'We'll go for a walk in the garden. It's so romantic at night, no?'

We walked out of thee room hand in hand, feeling thee needles from Tarzan's eyes making holes in our backsides.

'Enjoyed threesome?' Muesli asked, his big smile lighting not just his face, but entire breakfast area.

Tarzan rolled his eyes round round. Raj blinked his eyes. I *toh* closed my eyes.

It was thee morning after Tarzan had caught me between Raj's legs. Don't ask what-what happened after. Raj and I did go for short walk. But to thee Reception. Tried to get room. Begged Chusli to adjust. But no, *ji*, not. All rooms were booked for thee next two days. All Chusli could do was give was extra bed. And all of us spent night together in honeymoon suite. Tarzan and Raj in drawing room, me in bedroom.

'The boat's alive,' Muesli told Tarzan.

'My boat's arrived?' Tarzan repeated.

I sat up straight. 'You're going?' I asked hopefully.

'Only to Bangkok,' he replied, picking up his sunglasses and getting to his feet. 'Andeep wants a bachelor party to beat all bachelor parties.'

'*Huhn*,' I tossed my hairs back in proudy manner.

'Dingy's party is going to beat Andeep's. You should see the spinster parties Mahi organizes,' Raj boasted as if he'd seen all of them.

Hai, he was touching me so much. Acting like loyal BF.

'I did see one,' Tarzan said, bringing his eyes straight on me.

My heart started doing zumba steps. My blood started running like race horse.

'You know the one,' Tarzan said, his voice dropping.

Gooses came on my arms and legs and where not. My mouth became dry like sand.

'I *toh* organise so many parties,' I said in casual voice. 'Which-which will I remember?'

I was matching Raj in acting. Because I could never forget thee party Tarzan was talking about. My mind flew back to Delhi and that night. And I was lost in flashback again.

'This is thee last time I'm organizing spinster party for oldies,' I ate swear as another drunk Aunty grabbed Naren thee stripper's bum and shook it left and right.

I was not moral science teacher, but thee way some Aunties were behaving! Heights of being perverted. Hello, stripper was also someone's son.

I was resting drunkum-drunk Bride Aunty on thee sofa, when he cried, 'Help, *yaar*!'

I rushed to save poor Naren, badly tripping on Bride Aunty's pink feather. First I caught myself, then I caught Duryodhan Aunty. Around thee waist, feeling like bouncer at rowdy bar. 'Party's over, Aunty. Time to go home.'

I'd switched on thee lights one hour ago. But these people were not getting thee message. Drinking, dancing, misbehaving like anything.

'Letsch go,' Duryodhan Aunty protested, thrashing like octopus as I tried to control her. 'I was justsch trying to…justch trying to…'

I knew what she was justsch trying to do. Grabbing thee waistband of Naren's *langot* (oho, thee G string *chaddi*). Thee elastic stretched badly as I pulled Aunty back and her fingers had no choice but to leave it. The elastic went flying back to hit Naren loudly and painfully like whip.

'Owwww!' he cried.

'Owwww!' I cried as Duryodhan aunty sank her sharp nails in my arms.

'Letsch me go!' she yelled.

'Okay!' I yelled, removing my arms.

DHAMMMMM!

She fell down on thee floor like potato sack.

'Hey, you,' I clicked my fingers at another drunk Aunty who was kissing metal pole, thinking it was Naren, who else. 'Yes you, Emraan Hashmi, take your friend and go.'

I clapped my hands loudly.

She gave last *chumma* to thee pole and came stumbling-shumbling. She bent down and lifted her friend up with one hand. She balanced Duryodhan Aunty against thee wall, before reaching for her purse.

DHAMMMMMM!

Duryodhan Aunty tasted thee floor back again.

Other Aunty turned attention to bag and struggled with her opening – means, bag opening. She opened it, pulled out roll of folded notes and stuffed it inside thee stripper's G-string *chaddi*.

Uff!

I threw open thee door of thee flat and threw both Aunties out.

Then I ran to Naren. He was rubbing his bum, which was paining from all thee grabbing and pinching. I put my hand inside his G-string *chaddi*. My fingers had just grabbed thee roll of folded notes.

I realised that the idiot drunkard Aunties had left thee door open only when someone gasped loudly.

I turned around to see my Tarzan standing there. I was so shockum-shocked, my hand didn't come out of thee *chaddi*. Only guilty came on my face.

'Don't let me interrupt you,' he said in freezer cold voice, before doing about-turn.

'Lav, wait!'

He hesitated, his feet slowing hand.

'We've to drop thee strippe – we've to drop Naren home.'

Tarzan walked out of thee door, shutting it loudly behind him.

Syapa!

I knew, I knew it was bad idea to let him pick me after thee party. I should have taken Uber Ola back home. Oho, I wanted to. But he'd forced. Said it wasn't safe. That anyway he was working late. And Bride Aunty's flat was on thee way. So I was like okay okay, pick up.

On thee way back, there was cremation-ground-type silence. Tarzan was too angry to speak. Naren was too tired to speak. I was angry and tired and surprised. Angry because Tarzan was misunderstanding me. Tired because we were having too many fights. Over small small things only, but still. And surprised because, I never knew Tarzan was possessive. As if I could look at another hot man. I *toh* was very happy with my Hot Star (not app, BF).

After we dropped Naren home, I turned to my Angry Old Man. Told him PMS PMS PMS thousand and one times all thee way back. But he kept driving like silent film hero.

By thee time we reached home, my mercury was also high. He wanted me to fall on his feet or what? If he didn't want to talk to me, he could go die.

11

The one CBFC would have banned for more reasons than one

I marched to thee cupboard and purposely took out my night slip – thee short, satin, wine colour one with thin straps which he loved. *Hai*, thee look on his face when I came out of thee bathroom wearing it! My cheeks turned wine colour.

He'd already changed and gone inside blanket. But I could feel his eyes on me. I coolly walked to thee mirror opposite thee bed, brushed my hairs, rubbed night cream, hand cream, ignoring him. Then I went to my side of thee bed, climbed in, pulled thee blanket over my head and switched off thee side table lamp.

His side table got switched on.

I smiled inside thee blanket. I knew, I knew thee night slip would open his mouth.

'You want to talk?' He asked in swollen voice.

'About what?' I asked innocently from inside thee blanket.

'You know what.' He sat up and snatched thee blanket off.

'No, I don't know what,' I said, sitting up to face him.

'What if it was YOU who'd caught ME?'

'With your hand inside Naren's *chaddi*?' I imagined him doing that and it made me giggle.

'You think it's funny?' he growled.

'You, you're funny.'

He gave me dirty look.

'I told you sorry thousand and one times,' I reminded him. 'And what did you do? You showed me attitude. Let me tell you, I wasn't maaroing chance on Naren, okay? I was doing my job.'

'Your job is to fondle strippers?'

I gave him 'what's-wrong-with-you' look. 'Your mom asked me to plan spinster party for her friend, I did. Her friend asked me to organize stripper, I did. She asked me to be around, make sure thee party was rocking, I did. But all thee Aunties – they fond...fon...'

'Fondled,' Tarzan supplied.

'Fondled him too much,' I went on, 'so I had to—*had to*—jump in.'

'Yeah, why should guests have all the fun,' Tarzan said under his breath.

I made my eyes narrow. 'What did you say?'

'Nothing.'

'Anyways, do I mind what you do at your job, Lavith?'

'My job doesn't involve frisking people's underwear. And neither does yours, Mahi.'

'*Uff!* I told you sorry, *na*? What more do you want? Stop acting so "j". So what if Naren's hot? For me, he's only party prop.'

Thee corners of Tarzan's mouth went up.

'Party prop,' he went snort-snort.

I tucked my hairs behind my ears. 'I *toh* have said everything I wanted to say. Now you do what you want.'

Tarzan leaned forward, put his index fingers under thee thin straps of my night slip.

'What are you doing?' I asked.

'You said "do what you want",' he whispered, sliding them off my arms and bending down to kiss my shoulder.

I was still shivering from thee memory of that kiss and also everything that happened after that. If it'd happened in one of our Bollywood films, our Censor Board would have surely banned it.

Sadly, Tarzan clicked his fingers. My flashback was cut. I came back to thee present, to Hawa Hawai island, to thee breakfast table.

'Mahi, you there?' he asked.

'Y-Yes, yes,' I said, picking up thee butter knife and putting butter on my toast.

'What were you thinking about?'

I turned red like thee apple on thee table.

'Nothing, I wasn't thinking anything,' buttering my toast with more speed.

'Didn't she just butter her toast?' Tarzan asked Raj.

'She just buttered her toast,' Raj confirmed.

I threw down thee butter knife. *Hai*, I *toh* was losing my mental balance.

'Coming to Bangkok?' Tarzan asked. But not me, only Raj.

I was suspicious. Why was Tarzan acting kindly and offering day trip to my BF? Was his plan was to get thee truth out of Raj?

'Sorry, bro –' Raj began.

I showed him eyes. *Bro?* They spent one night together and became bros? What a party-changer he was!

'Sorry, Lavith,' Raj revised. 'But I'm here to help Mahi with wedding preparations. I'm her ass –'

I kicked Raj under thee table.

'He's acting like ass, but he's my new partner,' I announced. 'Dingy's going away after marriage, so...'

Luckily, Raj didn't jump up, shouting 'Really, Mahi, really'. But he looked so grateful, I was worried he'd fall on my feets and start kissing them.

'Whatever,' Tarzan said, lifting his shoulder. 'Need anything from Bangkok?'

Raj opened his mouth, but I kicked him under thee table again.

'No thanks, we don't want any favour.'

'I'm done being polite here,' Tarzan said, walking away angrily. 'Go to hell.'

'First you, then I.'

Raj looked at me first, then Tarzan, question marks on his face.

I told myself it was good only that Tarzan went to Bangkok. I told Muesli all my ideas. I told Raj to take notes. After Muesli promised to get contacts of all thee suppliers, he made suggestion. Day tour of Hawa Hawai island. On my first day, thee cheater-cock taxi-driver had given me unofficial *darshan* of thee island. Hand *ke* hand, I was going to say no. But I looked at my employee and changed my mind. He looked so excited, I didn't have thee heart to break his heart. He was working for me free, so like good boss, I negotiated free – means, part of wedding package – island discovery trip.

We took selfies enthusiastically at thee famous temples, we clapped encouragingly at thee Artist Village, we roamed about joblessly in thee vineyard, we watched sunset sighingly at hill with complicated name (Khao Shao something-something).

Actually, more than discovery of island, it was discovery of Raj. He wasn't hundred percent *laudu*, okay, okay maybe ten to twelve percent *laudu*. I was still little irritated because he'd pressurised me into giving him job. But he didn't ask me any questions about my personal life, he didn't question me when I gave him professional to-do list, he didn't even back-answer when I said no wine-tasting at thee vineyard.

We were going to check out thee last item on the iti…itin..oho, tour – Cicada Market – after quick stop at our resort.

'Someone waiting for you,' Chusli told us at the reception.

My face fell down. Tarzan was back. So was reality. For few hours, I'd felt like normal tourist, not heartbroken girl. Thee day had made me forget thee past. But evening had sent cruel reminder.

I followed Raj to thee room, my legs heavy.

Before we could ring thee bell, thee door opened.

And I died.

My friend hadn't arrived. Simran had!

'You!'

'You!'

We said at thee same time.

'What are you doing here?'

'What are you doing here?'

Again we said same thing, same time.

I turned to Raj, my eyes raining fire.

'I didn't know she was coming, I swear!' he cried in panic.

'Don't tell lies,' I looked at him like he was garbage truck.

'He's not lying,' Simran said.

'Who else knows you're here?' I demanded.

'No one. Our parents have gone to Canada,' she said, 'And I haven't spoken to Dumpy. I only spoke to our travel agent –'

'And he gave you family discount, so you jumped on thee plane and came here?' I said in acid voice.

In reply she burst out crying.

I stared at her, thinking what new *syapa* now. Then only I noticed that her under eyes area was dark and nose was red.

'Simran! Oye, what happened, Simran?' he asked, shaking her shoulder. 'Say something.'

One guest passing by stopped and gave concerned look to Simran. As if we were both attacking her.

'Let's take thee family drama inside,' I muttered, pushing thee twins into the room.

I made Simran sit on thee settee, made Raj serve her water (from complimentary bottle), made sure she knew why we came to Bangkok (not to take drugs, to plan Dingy's wedding), and then made her talk. I crawled to thee round pillow and rested my back. It was paining like anything.

'I came because I was stressed and sad,' she started, wiping her nose. 'Stressed because Raj had been acting very strange and I thought he was taking drugs –'

'What?' Raj cried, looking as if she'd driven truck over his leg.

Simran went on '…And sad because I don't know if Dumpy loves me.'

She came all thee way to Bangkok for that? I could have given her thee answer on thee phone. Oho, after I'd rejected Dumpy, he'd rebounded with her. How could anyone fall in love so soon…?

You fell in love in two weeks, my inside voice said. My heart twisted in all thee directions like rubberband. I felt sympathy wave rise up for Simran.

'You're older and wiser, Mahi,' she sob-sobbed, making my sympathy wave go back. 'You tell. Do you think he loves me?'

Hai, I *toh* didn't know what to say. I couldn't tell her thee truth. What if she was suicide-type like her brother? I'd go to jail for two two criminal cases. But I didn't want to lie to her also.

I'd seen Hollywood movie long back in which depress case goes to doctor for help. Asks him may questions. In thee name of helping, doctor asks him thee same questions. Patient answers them patiently. And both go home happy. Patient, because doctor solved his mental problem. Doctor, because patient solved his financial problem.

So like thee doctor, I asked her thee same question. 'You feel he doesn't love you?'

She nodded. 'He doesn't. Or why will he keep his own sister's wedding secret?'

'Because it's top secret!'

'If it's a secret, then why does Raj know?' she argued. 'And how can you have secrets from your GF?'

'You think BF-GFs should not have secrets?' I tried the same bull-and-cock tactic again.

'No, never!' Simran cried, crushing thee plastic bottle in her hand. 'Because that means they are not serious about each other. Dumpy's not serious about me. He doesn't tell me anything. He doesn't want me to attend his only sister's wedding. He doesn't want to introduce me to his family...'

Uff!

Simran should have been lawyer, because she raised one point after another.

'You tell me, Mahi, is that love?'

'It *toh* depends on your definition of love,' I gave safe, diplomatic, nonsense answer.

'What's your definition?' she asked, wiping her cheek.

'This I've got to hear,' came familiar voice from behind. 'Do tell.'

Uff!

Tarzan's timing also *na*.

I turned around slowly, but treated him like afternoon sun. Didn't look straight up at him.

'Simran, meet Lavith,' I started giving intros, hoping thee direction of conversation would change. 'Lavith, this is Simran, Raj's sister.'

Simran wiped her nose, thinking loudly. 'Lavith? Where did I hear this name recently...not common... but sounds familiar...wait, you're THAT Lavith? Mahi's Delhi boyfriend?'

Sauteli maa ki @#$%! That *chodu* Dumpy! Keeping ten thousand things secret from her, but opening his bloody mouth for this! And duffer Simran, opening her mouth in front of Tarzan.

Understanding came on Raj's face like tubelight, little late, little slowly but fully. 'He's Mahi's Delhi boyfriend?' He dropped down on thee settee like heavy potato sack.

Uff!

Dumpy had given my history to Raj also. I was going to give him solid when he landed in Bangkok.

'Famous am I?' Tarzan said walking up to us.

'World famous in Ludhiana,' I replied in acid voice.

'But what's he doing here?' Simran raised another good point.

'Do you want to do the honours, Ma-hee, or shall I?' Tarzan asked, offering his hanky to Simran. She took it, looking as if he'd given her Kohinoor diamond.

'It's long story, longer than Ashutosh Gowariker films. In short-cut version, Lavith helped in saving Andeep-Dingy's relationship. Andeep helped in saving Lavith's life. Lavith helped in booking this resort.'

Then I looked at Tarzan. '*Bas*, happy? Now please go. We're discussing private matter.'

Instead of listening to me, Tarzan came and made himself comfortable on thee settee as if it was public park.

'It's okay, it's only Lavith,' Simran said as if he they were *chaddi* buddy for donkey years. 'Let him be here. I don't mind.'

Tarzan gave me 'loser' look, before bringing back thee same topic. 'So, Mahi, you were going enlighten us all on the 'L' word.'

All eyes turned on me.

'First you, then I,' I snapped.

'I'm old school, you see. I always let the lady come first.'

He said it innocently, but the look in his eyes! *Saala*! As if I didn't understand his double meaning talks!

Simran raised her hand as if it was Britannia quiz contest.

'By all means,' Quizmaster Tarzan gave her permission.

'I think love means sharing and trusting. And not keeping secrets.'

'I think love is friendship –' Raj gave his expert opinion.

'Got that from a movie, buddy?' Tarzan teased.

'No! I swear!' Raj pinched his throat. 'What do you think, Mahi?'

All eyes turned to me, making me self-conscious.

'I don't want to play these stupid-type games,' I said, pushing my hairs back.

'Come on, Ma-hee, what are you afraid of?' Tarzan challenged.

Anyone who knew me this much also knew that thee word 'afraid' wasn't in my dictionary. I knew Tarzan was trying to provoke me. I knew he wanted to hear my answer, I knew it would be big mistake to attempt thee question. But Mahi Ahluwalia never left any battlefield like coward. She fought even when she was 100% sure she'd lose.

I took deep yoga breath. 'I *toh* don't know too much,' I said softly. 'I only know that love's love…pure, kind…it's not selfish…when you love someone, you don't think about yourself…you think about thee other person, what they like, what they want, what makes them happy…so that's my definition…love means making someone happy. Even if it makes you unhappy, even if it breaks your heart –'

Uff!

How much was I talking! I shut my mouth in middle of thee sentence. Simran was so touchum-touched, she started crying again. Raj looked as if I'd given thee answer to all thee problems in thee universe's problems, free. Tarzan, I *toh* didn't dare to look at.

My eyes went to him only when Raj asked, 'And what do you think, bro?'

His face, it looked deep fried with anger. As if I'd done surgical strike on him. I stopped breathing. I badly wanted to hear his answer. I knew I was acting like one stupid. As if his answer would be 'Love means having feelings for someone even after they leave you without giving notice'.

Tarzan swung his legs off the bed, looking at me and only at me, and spat out thee words, 'I think you're full of shit.'

And in few long steps, he was out of thee room.

12

The one with the (mistaken) identity crisis

'Where's Lavith?' Simran asked, her eyes looking over my shoulder.

Why was she asking me, I was his secretary or what? I peesoed my teeth, getting into thee boat. Already my head was paining. Because of Simran, I was going to get tooth pain also.

'He's not coming,' she said in disappointed voice as thee engine started.

'If you want, you can stay back too,' I said sweetly.

Arre, we were going to Bangkok for work, not for bloody picnic. Muesli had given contact of one panditji and one more secret supplier. It was surprise for Andeep-Dingy and I didn't know if Raj-Simran could keep things in their stomachs.

Muesli had given idea for calm and quiet Thai wedding also. Said he'd arrange everything – from Buddhist priest who'd conduct thee ceremony to special tailor who'd stitch traditional Thai costumes for Dingy and Andeep.

But thee problem with us Punjabis is, if we don't wear fancy dress, if our drunk relatives don't dance with whiskey glasses on top of heads, if we don't have multi-cuisine buffet counters, if panditji doesn't chant mantras we cannot understand, we don't feel married.

'Mahi, I've made a list of questions we can ask Panditji,' Raj said, tapping thee notepad with pencil.

I peesoed my teeth again. I liked to collect stationery (and also toiletry) from hotels and resorts. That's why I saved them till thee last day. But Raj had used them. They were totally spoilt now. He was more than fifteen percent *laudu*.

As thee boat jumped over thee waters, my breakfast jumped into my throat. I closed my eyes and took deep breaths. I didn't know what was making me irritated – thee boat ride or what had happened last night.

Tarzan had accused me of fully shitting. *Arre*, why would I shit in front of everyone? What award would I get for telling lies? I was trying to indirectly tell him that whatever I was doing, was for thee sake of his happiness. That it was making me very sad, but it was for his own good. But he hadn't believed one word. No, *ji*, not.

At dinner, he hadn't said one word. He'd sat on our table, but his eyes were on his cell phone, his mind thousand miles away. Thee atmosphere in Lembla had become more polluted than Delhi in December.

Thank god, Dingy and Andeep were coming thee next day. And two days after that, Dumpy and all thee families. At least thee pollution levels would come down little bit.

I sighed and tried to concentrate on work. I took peek at Raj's notepad. 'Do you have any questions?'

Simran raised her hand. Oho, she hadn't come out of her classroom mentality.

'Ya, Simran?'

'Where does Lavith work?' she asked, trying to sound casual. But her cheeks were red tomatoes.

Uff! Tarzan had given her his hanky, not his heart.

He quit his bank job and is *vela* (oho, jobless) I wanted to say.

But I decided to answer her question with another question, 'Why? You're planning to hire him or what?'

'Lavith's started his own company,' Raj dropped bomb.

I sat up straight – means, as straight as possible in bouncy boat.

'Not party-planning company, I hope,' I said half-jokily.

We lived in different cities, but still, I didn't want him as competition. His mother father had too many contacts and he'd easily...

'He invests in startups – new businesses.'

I sent thanks to God in thee sky.

Looked like Raj had mugged up everything about Tarzan's company.

'Gives them consultation, opportunities, mentoring. He was anyways investing money for other people, making them rich in his old job –'

'Now he was going to invest his own money and make himself rich,' Simran completed.

I'd stopped listening to them. Thousand and one emotions were fighting for space inside me like people in third-class compartment of trains.

I felt excited, happy, proud. Tarzan had taken big step. He was finally doing what he always wanted to do.

I was cent percent sure his company would do *chutti* of competition.

I felt upsetted, hurted, insulted. He'd not bothered to share thee good news with me. He'd told Raj, his sleeping partner of two days. But kept it secret from his sleeping partner of many months.

Who had encouraged him – okay, okay, who had fought with him—to quit his job? Me. Who had advised him – okay, okay, shouted at him—to go behind his dreams? Me.

One of our discussions – okay, okay fight, on thee subject came to my head. I flashbacked back to Delhi.

It was Sunday. Tarzan was working. But I was paying thee price. I cursed his boss, his bank, his job, everything and everyone, for spoiling one more weekend.

Instead of burning blood unnecessarily, I thought why not do some cleaning-sheaning? It would bring thee dust plus my temperature down. So I changed into my old white Patiala salwar and faded flowery kurta. Tied my hairs up on head and my dupatta below eyes.

Then I cut Tarzan's purple tee shirt, the one I hated. Oho, not because I was angry with him, because I wanted new dusting cloth. If I'd used thee one our maid was using, I'd have made thee furniture more dirty. It was so old, so old, bets it was Dhiren Uncle's childhood tee shirt.

TING TONG! TING TONG!

I left dusting thee dining area in the middle and went to open door. Two old ladies were standing there.

'Lavith Sahni?' Oldy Number-One asked in doubtful 'Have-I-come to-thee-right-address' voice.

I nodded, pulling dupatta down from my nose. They looked like they had come straight after robbing jewellery store. Thee way diamonds were shining from all their body parts, I *toh* needed sunglasses.

'May we come in?' Oldy Number-Two asked.

Immediately, I was alerted. Why did they want to come inside thee flat? What if they were robbers/attackers/kidnappers? Part of big gang that rang bells of innocent people and robbed/attacked/kidnapped them? Wasn't there a write up in *Gurgaon Times* about *Buddhiya* (oho, oldy lady) Gang?

I quickly slammed thee door on their faces, put security chain and then put my neck out.

'Why?' I asked.

Oldy number One put her hand inside her bag.

Immediately, I was tense. She was taking out her gun! *Hai*, Oldy Aunty had no heart. She was going to kill me in full *jawani*. She'd seen life, done full *masti*, become ripe, but I, I was youngy-young. *Hai*, I *toh* hadn't told Tarzan sorry for fighting with him like anything in thee morning.

'No! Wait – don't,' I cried in panic, closing my eyes instead of door.

I watched in slow motion as her hand came out with gun…

'I'm Rachna, Neeru's friend. I wanted to give Lavith my son's wedding card.'

No gun! Card! There was wedding card in her hand. I almost fell down with relief. Same time my memory bell rang. Article in thee *Gurgaon Times* was about *Buddy* Gang. *Hai*, simply only I'd called them criminals.

I took thee card from her fingers. Then I took thee chain out and opened door wide. As wide as my smile. 'You're welcomed.'

They stepped inside, looking around.

'Come, come,' I pointed to sofa.

'Lavith's not home?' They asked sitting down.

'Lavith's gone to office,' I replied, sitting down on thee sofa opposite them.

Like all normal humans, Aunties looked fully surprised. *Arre*, who worked on Sunday?

'Is he expected back anytime soon?'

That's it. All my frustration came up to my mouth and I exploded. 'Only God knows. Actually, not even God knows. I *toh* have stopped expecting anything from him. I'm *toh* tired of thee same shit. I also work – I've been working for thee last six years. But this is too much –'

Thee Aunties looked shockum-shocked at my frank talks.

'Anyways, leave. What will you have to drink? Tea, coffee, juice? There's beer also.'

Thee Aunties looked at each other, funny expressions on their faces. *Hai*, so sweet, they were feeling shy, drinking in front of someone half their age.

'Don't worry, Aunties,' I winked. 'You don't tell anyone, I won't tell anyone.'

I walked to thee fridge and grabbed three cans of Heineken. I was going to throw thee cans at them, helpless from habit. Then I remembered. They were old. And they were guests. I picked up plate from thee dining table and used it as tray to serve thee Aunties.

I went and sat opposite them on thee sofa.

'Have, have,' I encouraged, putting my feet up. I opened thee can, and took one sip. 'Mmm, heaven,' I sighed. 'After all thee cleaning, I badly needed this.'

Thee Aunties jumped to their feet. 'We – we've got to leave –'

'Why, what happened? Have beer, *yaar*, give me company…'

Thee Aunties were old, but with what speed they reached thee door. They shut it behind their backsides, not bothering to look back.

'And they call thee youth rude and mannerless,' I grumbled, gulping down thee beer.

By thee time Tarzan came home, thee flat was shining. My mood was better. I'd taken long bath, shampooed, worn new night-suit and was feeling fresh.

'Hello, Mr. Hard,' I smiled, before naughtily adding, 'worker.'

Instead of replying, he sat down on thee sofa, put his legs on thee centre table and switched on the TV.

I sat down next to him.

Loud crying came from thee TV.

'Every single time. Some *fucked up* serial or the other,' he grumbled, pressing thee remote.

Nothing happened. Same channel stayed on screen.

'God, why won't this shit ever work?' he growled, pressing it harder.

Along with loud crying, woman on TV started beating her chest too.

'Fuck! Fuck! Fuck!' He hit thee remote hard against his palm three times and pointed it. Still same channel.

'Now what will you do, Mr. *Phoren* Returned?' I snatched thee remote.

'Not now, Mahi,' he snapped, pulling away, 'I'm not in the mood.'

'You're never in thee mood,' I said in same tone. 'I told you, quit your job, start your dream company. But no. See how frustrated you are.'

'Can you blame me? I haven't exactly been sitting on my arse, chilling all day –'

Bas, I couldn't take it anymore. Thief was scolding thee police.

'Neither have I, okay? I dusted thee whole flat –'

'Great, spoil Vimala some more, why don't you…'

Vimala was our maid. Sorry, our domestic help. Tarzan always kept telling me 'be politically correct, be politically correct'.

'Poor thing, she also needs break-shake,' I said in sympathy.

'God, do you even know what she's up to behind you back, Mahi?'

My ears went up. 'What?'

'Apparently, she drinks in our absence.'

'Vimala?' I *toh* couldn't believe. She was not thee type. At least, she didn't look like boozard.

'Yeah,' Tarzan continued. 'And the woman has expensive taste. Heineken beer, no less…'

Tarzan was so hysterical, he didn't notice my expression change. Understanding look came in my eyes.

'I used to wonder…the beer always seemed to disappear from the fridge…I mean, the cans don't drink themselves… mystery solved…and get a load of this… woman's got a problem with my working hours…what a fucking joke…bitches about my working hours to our guests, can you imagine? Precisely what she did this afternoon.' He turned to look at my tomato face. 'You'd stepped out?'

I sat with zip lips.

'Wait a minute,' Tarzan frowned. 'Isn't it Vimala's day off from work…did she…?' He didn't complete thee sentence. He took thee facts, did fast addition in his head and gave me 'I don't believe this' look.

'Oh!' He said at last, 'they thought *you* were…'

I knew I was badly dressed, but who dresses like queen and sits at home?

'*Hai*,' I cried out, 'how could they think I was thee *mai* – domestic help. How, how, how?'

Tarzan started looking uncomfortable. 'I don't know.' But his eyes told another story. So he thought it was easy to make that mistake?

'*Sauteli ma ki @#$%! Bhons@#$! Chu!@#$*' I burst.

'The way you talk, Mahi –'

I was so shockum-shocked, words got stuck in my throat, world turned upside down, heart stopped beating. Tarzan was saying that Aunties thought I was thee maid because of the way I *talked*? Because of my English, because of my accent, because I wasn't as educated as *him*? *Hai*, I *toh* never knew he thought like that.

'I didn't know you were ashamed of me, Lavith,' I said quietly.

'What? What the hell are you talking about?'

'My English, you're embarra –'

'What nonsense, I never said that,' he denied it thoroughly. 'I know you're spoiling for a fight, Mahi, but –'

My heavy heart squeezed like wet towel and water started coming out from my eyes. But I wasn't going to cry, not over something stupid like this. Ya, Tarzan was hi-fi, but I was no *paindu* (oho, loser-shoser). I was from different world, he was from different world. That's it. I never thought I was lesser than him. Or anyone else in thee bloody world. And in my dreams also I never thought he was ashamed of me.

'I never knew you were so judgemental, Lavith. So what if I can't do *chutter-putter* in perfect English? As if you're perfect –'

'Don't you dare project your shit on to me. If you're so bloody conscious about your diction, take bloody classes or something –'

Bas, my self-control's dam broke.

'You're a bastard! Bastard, bastard, bastard! That's what you are!' I shouted, before I could stop myself.

His face, it changed – became small, white, blank – in one second flat. That's when I realised. *Hai*, I *toh* was only giving him English *gaali*. But he'd misunderstood. He thought I was taunting him about his past. *Arre*, why would I blame him for what his father had done? What was his fault in that? He was poor innocent child trapped in thee middle of *tatti* life.

That's why, that's why mother-tongue *gaalis* are the best. They don't create confusion.

Thee boat bounced up suddenly and that was thee end of my flashback.

'Mahi, are you okay?' Raj asked, looking at me with concern.

I nodded, scared to speak. I didn't want to burst like water balloon in front of them.

To make thee matters more worse, last night's conversation came inside my head. Simran had felt bad because Dumpy had kept many things secret. I'd not taken her complain seriously then, but now I understood how she felt.

I was just like Simran. Thee only difference was that Simran loved Dumpy openly. And I cared for Tarzan hidingly. Oho, why to lie, I was in mad in Tarzan's love. So what if we couldn't be together? My feelings for Tarzan would always remain thee same. Yesterday, today, tomorrow, next birth.

Bas, I couldn't control anymore. My feelings came up from my heart and reached my eyes, making them watery.

'Are you crying?' Simran asked, inspecting my face like Masterchef inspects junior's dish.

'Mad or what?' I gave fake laugh, quickly wiping my eyes. 'It's thee salty air, it's hitting my eyes.'

Simran gave me understanding look and hanky. Thee same hanky Tarzan had given to her. I took it and touched it to my eyes.

She put her hand out after I finished, but I dropped it on my lap. Oho, not because I didn't want another girl to have Tarzan's hanky, because I wanted to reuse it later.

'Look, we've reached,' I distracted her, pointing at thee land ahead.

Simran clapped, looking more excited than Mister Columbus when he reached Um-reeca.

13

The one with the heart to heart and chest to chest

I was more tired than Sumo wrestler after big fight, but I was satisfied. Thee day trip to Bangkok had been success on professional and personal front. I'd met and locked Pandtiji, given him thee advance. Raj had taken notes like he was going to appear for Assistant Training Exam. Simran had shopped like malls were getting banned from the next day.

We reached thee resort late in thee evening. Raj fell down in thee drawing room, oho, on thee settee. Simran and her shopping bags fell down in thee bedroom. I fell over thee wash-basin in thee bathroom.

KNOCK! KNOCK!

'Room service.'

'Who ordered room service?' I asked, walking out of thee loo in bath gown. 'Not me.'

KNOCK!KNOCK!

We'd eaten dinner and come. But I knew about Raj and Simran. Their stomachs were like wells. How much ever food you threw inside, they were still empty.

'Not me,' Simran replied, busy trying thee clothes and admiring herself in thee mirror.

Raj didn't answer, he busy snoring loudly. Good, I thought, let Tarzan suffer at night. I wasn't doing competition, baba, but ya, I was much better sleeping partner than Raj.

'We didn't order room –' I opened thee door.

And died.

'Surprise!' Dumpy yelled, throwing his hands around me and picking me up.

'Dumpy! Put me down!'

In reply he started making circles. It was his lucky day *ki* I didn't vomit my whole dinner on his head.

'The lady asked you to put her down,' came quiet voice.

Uff!

Tarzan had come like public holiday on Sunday. At very wrong time.

Dumpy made one last circle and put me down.

They looked at each other like candidates fighting for thee same Lok Sabha seat.

Uff!

After I'd made *chutiyapa*-type mistake of proposing to Dumpy last year, they had become like Kejri and NaMo.

'Dumpy!' Simran gasped, stepping out of thee room. 'You? Here?'

'Oyee, my laddoo, barfi, jalebi, I was missing you,' he sang, rushing to her.

'But how did you know I was in Bangkok?'

'I found out from our travel agent,' Dumpy said proudly, like he'd come first in IIT entrance exam.

I wanted to take flight to Ludhiana, give their travel
agent *chittars* (oho, beating) and come back. *Khotta!*
Sending everyone to Thailand.

Dumpy picked Simran up and started going round
and round.

'Is that his standard greeting?' Tarzan said in Phenyl
voice, 'Or does he reserve that enthusiasm for the girls
he's crushing on?'

I gave Tarzan one elbow shot in his hard stomach.

'Shhh!' I said under my breath, showing him eyes.

It was thee truth. Dumpy's needle used to be stuck
on me. And that's why Simran used to act like sweet
knife with me. Thanks to God, we'd became – oho, not
friends, but civilised with each other. But she still had
STD (Suspense, Tension, Depression) thanks to Dumpy
and I didn't want her to get insecure about me again.

Raj came out of thee room, rubbing his eyes. 'What's
all the noise?'

'Ludhiana Reunion,' Tarzan told him.

'Dumpy?' Raj blinked as Dumpy put Simran down.

'Way to keep the elopement a secret, guys,' Tarzan
muttered. 'What next? The entire *baraat* two days early?'

I was also bugged up. First Raj, then Simran, then
Dumpy. This was conducted tour of Thailand or what?

Didn't they understand anything? Or they
understood everything but didn't care? We had to – *had
to* – keep Dingy and Andeep's elopement secret. Okay,
fine, Raj and Simran were outsiders, but what about
Dumpy? Why was he acting like duffer and risking
exposing thee truth?

'Don't worry, Mahi, nothing will happen,' Raj said
putting arm around me like loving BF.

He should have stopped there, but did overacting
like SRK and kissed my head also.

Two mouths fell down. Dumpy's. Simran's. One mouth became thin line. Tarzan's.

I was too tired to take Dumpy or Raj's class, so I marched inside thee room without wishing anyone good night. But Bhooto's '*Hai hai* note-ban' WhatsApps didn't let me sleep.

Next morning, Baadshah (not king, rap singer) beat Bhooto in waking me up. He was singing *Chull, ladki kar gayi chull* outside thee bedroom. I sat up straight and stretched my body. Simran kept sleeping like she was dead body.

I went out to find Dumpy hunting for his phone.

Uff!

Him and his ring tone. Always on maximum volume.

But Raj was selling horses and sleeping like his sister.

'Must be Dingy or Andeep,' he said, checking under thee carpet. 'To tell that they are boarding…'

For thee first time in I don't how many months – okay, okay two months – I felt little excited. Wedding was coming! So was Dingy! And extra room! I'd become Dingy's roommate. I *toh* didn't care who else slept where and with whom.

Thee day passed in fast forward.

Ludhiana Brigade ate, drank, swam, went to spa, slept. I ate, slept, and avoided being alone with Dumpy (oho, I didn't want to answer any question on thee Raj topic). God only knew what Tarzan did. He was missing all day. Waiting to make entry at thee wrong time I was sure.

But he made entry in thee evening, along with Dingy and Andeep. Then only I realised that he'd gone to Bangkok and returned after picking them up. I felt irritated means irritated. Thee resort had arranged airport pick up, it was part of thee wedding package. So why was he jumping so much? Trying to show he was thee better wedding-planner or what?

Dingy yelled, 'Mahi-ve!' and ran up to hug me and I forgot all my irritation.

'I'm getting married! To Andeep! In Bangkok!' Dingy sang, 'I still can't believe.'

Leave married, I *toh* still couldn't believe she could fall in love with Andeep. But why to start old topic, I thought, patting my pillow. I was happy I'd made her mine – means, I'd made her my roommate and we were talking late at night, just like we used to in our bachelor days...I slapped my forehead as I remembered something.

'*Arre*, before I forget, you're sure you want to combine your bachelor party with Andeep?'

She nodded. 'I'd sent you, *na*, WhatsApp before leaving India?'

'Ya, ya, but did you talk to Andeep? What if he wants–'

'Andeep wants what I want, Mahi-ve,' she cut me. 'He doesn't want same boring Bangkok-type of bachelor party – boys only, going to strip club, drinking till morning. We'll all go to Bangkok tomorrow evening and party-sharty. Then we'll come back and party-sharty with families. Okay?'

Girl side, boy side, my side, everyone was reaching thee next day.

'Hmm.'

Tarzan had been planning big bachelor party in Bangkok. But now he'd be stuck with me. Means, with all of us. Good, I thought with satisfaction. Oho, not because I didn't want him to have fun with Bangkok girls, because I didn't want him to corrupt young Indian boy, Raj. Dumpy *toh* could corrupt God also. Andeep I was least bothered about.

'Mahi, shall I tell you one secret?' Dingy's voice interrupted my thoughts.

I gave her headmaster-type look.

'What did you do now, Dingy? Did you do *chumma-chaati* with Rajinder before coming to Bangkok?'

Rajinder, her BF before Andeep. He was Mr. One Way Traffic. Even after Dingy had stopped giving him green signal, he kept driving on her road.

'*Chee!* I could never do kissy-ussy with anyone!'

'Why,' I asked in sly voice, 'you're not horn dog or what?'

Thee hero of our first colourful experience – oho, first adult film we'd seen together – had kept calling himself 'horndog'. He had thee sex-wala disease. Twenty-four hours he thought only of one thing – sex. Morning to night, he did it with girls, boys, himself. He *toh* didn't leave his furniture also.

We both burst into giggles.

Hai, what golden days they were.

'Mahi-ve , please don't mind, but I was always little jealous of you.'

'What?' I cried, sitting up straight. I thought I knew everything about Dingy. But she'd kept such big secret from me.

'Calm down, Mahi,' she told my dialogue to me, pulling me back down.

'But why Dingy why?'

I wasn't richum-rich or beauty queen or scholar type.

'Because you're you, Mahi. Always so confident, so bold, so brave...'

I opened my mouth to say no-no, but then I thought why to lie?

'...you've always been thee centre of attraction. With teachers, with boys, with clients. Everywhere we go, people talk only about you, your good qualities...'

That was also true. But I'd equal number of bad qualities.

'...Please don't misunderstand me, Mahi,' she said, sitting up. 'I love you –'

'I know...more than you love Andeep...you told me –'

'...But I–I always came after you. Mahi first, Dingy second...'

Life's not a race, Dingy, I wanted to say. But I couldn't open my mouth.

'That's why sometimes I used to feel jealous...' Dingy finished, looking at me with worried eyes. 'Say something, Mahi-ve.'

I *toh* didn't know what to say. Never in my life, I thought my best friend was jealous of me. I wanted to cry.

'...I was hundred percent sure that you'd get married first...and when Lavith came into your life, I became doubly sure –'

'Forget all that,' I said quickly, before I became senti. 'You don't feel second now?'

'No, no...' she said, putting her hand on mine, 'now I feel so special...I'm Dingy – thee bride...it sounds like name of cool film, *na*?...I'm so happy everyone's talking about me, my marriage...'

'I'm so happy, too.' And I meant it from heart. If Dingy was happy marrying Andeep, I was happy. I ate swear that I'd try my best to like – okay, okay– I'd try my best to tolerate him. For her sake.

I leaned forward and gave her tight-shight hug.

'I'm so stupid,' I slapped my forehead suddenly as I remembered something.

'What happened, Mahi-ve?' Dingy asked, taking her hands off.

'I forgot my med…I forgot something in my old room,' I said, climbing out of thee bed.

'What?'

'Only you can have secrets or what?' I said, jokily. 'I'll get it and come in five minutes. Don't sleep, okay?'

I still had one room card. I took it out of my handbag and went to thee old room, my heart feeling heavy and light at thee same time. Heavy, because for so many years, I didn't know Dingy felt 'j' of me. Light, because, now she didn't feel 'j' of me.

I opened thee door, ready to say sorry to Dumpy and Raj for disturbing their sleep. Copying me, Tarzan had also moved out of thee suit and into Andeep's room. But thee sitting area was empty. I went to thee bedroom door and knocked softly. There was no reply. Thinking Simran was fast asleep, I turned thee handle and walked in.

And *died*.

Simran was not asleep! She was not alone! She was in Tarzan's arms!

I *toh* couldn't believe what I saw. They were standing chest to chest. Tarzan was like thee jeeps in Ludhiana. Topless. He was wearing only his small-sholl, tight-shight shorts. She was wearing night-gown: but it had slipped from her shoulders. She'd made kissy face and was looking up at him.

My whole world turned upside down. I'd thought I didn't care who slept where and with whom. *Hai*, I was wrong.

I *toh* don't know what I did. Whether I gasped loudly or gave *gaali* in Hindi and Punjabi and English. But I think so I made some noise, because they gasped loudly and gave *gaali*. In Hindi and Punjabi and English.

I stood there for one second like dumb, frozen, statue, before doing instant about-turn and running out of thee bedroom.

'Mahi! Wait!' I heard Tarzan call out.

But I wasn't mad to. I went running to my new room and slammed thee door.

'Mahi, what hap – ?' Dingy asked, sitting up on thee bed as I locked thee door and stood behind it.

'Mahi! I said open up!' Tarzan barked, hitting thee door. 'Mahi! Listen to me.'

I signalled to Dingy to stay on thee bed, tears flowing down my cheeks.

'I don't want to hear anything.'

Dingy looked very concerned but she listened to me.

'Mahi, I can explain.'

'I don't want any explanation! GO DIE!'

'MAHI!'

Tarzan banged thee door many times, but I didn't listen to him. I went back to thee bed only when I heard his footsteps going away.

'Mahi, what happened –?'

'I don't want to talk about it and spoil everything... please, *yaar*...this time...this trip, this occasion...it's about you and only you, Dingy.'

And I'd make sure it would be, I ate swear, getting into bed.

Dingy went to sleep in minutes, but I *toh* couldn't. I felt so cheap, so stupid. I was duffer queen to love animal like Tarzan. He'd never loved me. If he had, could he have action scene with someone else only two months after our breakup? No, *ji*, not.

And what about Simran? She didn't have breakup with Dumpy. How could she do to this to him? Was she trying to take revenge on me? But what was my fault if her BF used to have one eye on me?

Anyways, Simran was third party. If your own coin is fake, why to blame another person? Tarzan was thee bigger culprit.

I don't know how I got sleep, but next morning another shock was waiting for me. My medicine pouch – thee thing I'd gone to get from thee room – was on thee side table.

I picked it up, forgetting to breathe.

Dingy came out of thee loo, patting her face with towel. 'Simran came to give it to you.'

I got tensed. Had she looked inside? I looked into Dingy's eyes, but her expression was innocent. Thanks to god.

But what about Simran?

14

In which hearts etcetera are stripped open and feelings etcetera are laid bare

'Mahi, how can you look so bored, *yaar*? I'm *toh* so excited, so excited, I can't explain you.' Dingy squeezed Andeep's hand, looking up at thee stage.

Tell that to your fiancé, I wanted to reply.

We were sitting inside thee third night club of thee evening and watching thee performances. Andeep was looking like he was having root canal surgery at Chaddha Dental clinic. *Arre*, it was his fault. Who asked him to cancel his old plan and have combo bachelor party with Dingy?

I never like to praise my competition, but Tarzan had planned everything like professional. Instead of bachelor night, he'd made it bachelor overnight. Booked suite with two bedrooms in Bangkok hotel and organised two taxis for two whole days. But highlight was thee lunch at cool-shool restaurant called Cabbages and Condoms. When bill came, so did free condoms for every customer! I *toh* wanted to suggest thee same idea for Bhooto's next lunch kitty. My mood became slightly okay imagining thee expressions of all Aunties.

'Enough, *yaar*, Dingy,' I complained.

Oho, not because I was bored of seeing girls and wanted to see boys in short-short *chaddis* dancing with their long poles. Because thee next day was thee *Sangeet*, and I wanted to make sure all arrangements were perfect.

'Last dance,' she promised. 'Say cheese, *yaar*,' she said clicking selfie.

But I couldn't smile or enjoy or act normal because I couldn't stop thinking about last night. I looked at thee other two parties from last night. They were sitting in thee first row, opposite to us, looking normal. Simran was sticking to Dumpy like anything, Tarzan was drinking like anything. It was so easy for them, acting like nothing had happened.

I looked at Dumpy. He was dressed in khaki shorts and black tee shirt, looking like Shikari Shambhu going for hunting. Thee poor thing was rotating his hand above his head, not knowing his GF was rotating between him and another man. For thee first – okay, okay for thee second time (first time was when I'd broken my engagement with him)– in my life I felt really sorry for him.

My eyes went to Tarzan. He was dressed in blue jeans, white shirt and jacket, looking like HPM (oho, Hot *Phoren Munda*). *Kutta!* He didn't even have thee decency to look like thee *kameena* he was.

Unfortunately, he looked at me at thee same time. I turned to my right side, put my hand on Raj's shoulder and whispered in his ear. Oho, not because I wanted to make Tarzan jealous, because Raj was two beers down.

He'd reached his maximum quota. 'Enough, time to go, Raj.'

'No!' He pushed my hand away and continued drinking. Tarzan gave me fake smile and raised his whiskey glass in silent 'cheers'. I gave him my 'go die' look.

I pulled up my deep neck self-consciously. I was wearing Indo-Western outfit that I'd specially got stitched for Dingy's wedding. Sleeveless black *kameez* with buttons till navel, long front slit and high side slits. My bottom – means, my outfit's bottom was golden cigarette pants. Luckily, they had elastic band.

I was still adjusting my outfit when one beautiful stripper with long glim-glim hairs, jing-jing dress, shim-shim make-up, came and sat down on Dumpy and started doing lap dancing. Simran jumped up from her seat, covered her mouth and started giggling. Dumpy *toh* looked like he'd won Punjab State Lottery.

After giving him thee dance of his life, she turned to Tarzan. *Bas*, I reached my maximum limit. I *toh* couldn't sit there anymore. I jumped to my feet and rushed straight to thee exit.

My heart stopped beating, my stomach started churning like washing-machine. It was *toh* thee limit only. I'd seen Tarzan robbing fun – Part One with Simran. I couldn't bear to see Part Two with stripper.

I wasn't going to wait for anyone anymore – oho, thee families would be waiting at thee resort – but everyone (except Tarzan) came out in one minute.

'What happened, Mahi?' everyone asked together. 'What happened?'

'I'm going back to thee hotel,' I said, walking away. 'You all can stay here till morning. Bye.'

I sounded calm, but inside I was like sea in high tide. Tarzan had stayed back in thee club. He'd done lap dancing on my face, what only he'd do behind my backside?

I knew it was not my business, I knew he wasn't my BF, I knew I couldn't tell him anything, but who would tell all that to my deaf heart.

'I'll come with you,' Dingy said.

It was Andeep's turn to look like he'd won thee lottery.

'Andeep, you're coming?'

He looked like it was time for another root canal surgery, but he said, 'Yes, yes, *jaanu*. Would I let you go alone, in taxi, in strange city?'

Three of us got into of thee rented taxis. I didn't say one word on thee way back.

I know that self-praise is donkey praise, but thee arrangements were superb means superb. I'd stood on Muesli's head all afternoon and made sure they followed all my instructions.

There was floral arch leading into thee Riverside Verandah. Thee furniture had been removed and thee floor had been covered with mattresses and white sheets. There were twinkle lights on thee ceiling, jasmine curtains on thee sides and lamps hanging on thee corners. Waiters were carrying big silver trays and serving snacks. Everyone was singing, dancing, drinking, eating, enjoying.

I'd brought Bathinda to Bangkok, *ji*.

'Did you get thee *dholki*?' I asked Niku.

Arre, our Punjoo Sangeets aren't complete without beating our drum.

'You'd let me live if I forgot?' he smiled. 'I'll go to my room and –'

'Give me both keys, room and bag,' I said, blocking his way. 'I'll go and get.'

Not only because he'd landed only two hours before and needed rest, but also because I wanted to have my folic acid, multivitamins and Digene tablets.

'Don't miss thee chicken satay,' I reminded him.

I stopped for few minutes in my room, before going to Niku's room. I picked up thee instrument and was going to leave, when sound came from the loo.

I wasn't alone! Thee room wasn't empty! Someone was in thee loo!

If everyone was at thee Riverside Verandah, who was inside? My heart beating like drum, I lifted thee *dholki* over my head, ready to throw it at thee robber/ murderer/rapist's head. In slow motion, I saw thee loo door handle turn. And out came – *hayo rabba* – Tarzan. For one second, he looked at me like I was robber/ murderer/rapist.

'Interesting weapon of choice, Mahendar,' he said at last, looking up at thee *dholki*.

'What are you doing here?' I asked.

'Niku wanted this.' He brought up his hands to show the bottle of Savlon.

Immediately, I became worried. 'What happened to Niku?' I asked, bringing my hands down.

'Calm down, he's fine. Pammi Aunty tripped.'

Bhooto had hurt herself?

Uff!

Without imaginary health problems, she created so much scene, with real one, God only knew what she'd do.

'I'll go and check,' I spinned around to walk out of thee room.

In few long steps, he reached me and grabbed my hand.

'Not so fast.'

'Leave my hand,' I twisted it right and left, struggling to free it.

He didn't leave me. I also didn't leave him. I dropped thee *dholki* on his foot.

'OWWWW!' He cried out, hopping on one foot. 'What did you do that for?'

I couldn't say For-all-thee-dirty-things-you-did-last-night- *kutte*, so I gave him fake PMS (oho, how many times to tell – Please Mistake Sorry) look.

I turned to open thee door but his big hand fell on it.

'Why did you walk out of the night club, Mahi?' he asked.

'I wasn't feeling well.' I turned to give solid look.

'I see. What happened?' The way he looked into my eyes! As if he could see inside my chest and know the truth.

'I–I don't know.'

He could see inside my chest because next second he said, 'Perhaps the thought of someone else giving me a lap dance made you feel sick?'

He grabbed my hand again and moved his thumb softly on my wrist. *Bas*, my entire body started going buzz-buzz-buzz like cell phone on vibrator mode.

'Have you seen your face in thee mirror?' I lied in brave voice. 'Why should I care about who you do *chak dhoom dhoom* with?'

'*Chak* what?' he asked, leaning towards me, covering me with his deo, his perfume.

I hadn't touched alcohol in months, but I started feeling badly dehydrated.

'*Chak dhoom dhoom.*' I licked my lips and his burning eyes fell on them. 'It means –'

'I know what it means.' he said softly as his hand slowly moved up my arm. 'But I wasn't...'

My heart started doing acrobatics as if it was in bloody Russian Circus.

'Wasn't what?' I asked, but not with too much hope.

'...doing *chak dhoom dhoom* with the stripper,' he continued. 'Wasn't interested...'

Hai, I *toh* felt so relieved my legs felt weak. I wanted to fall on thee ground, fold my hands and scream, 'Thank you, *Rabba!*' But I controlled.

'But you, baby,' his voice went low, making me all tingle tingle, 'you can give me a lap dance anytime you want –'

'No, never,' I ate swear.

But my eyes, my hands, my heart said, 'Yes, always'.

'So why don't I buy it, Mahi? Just like I don't buy that little silly story you cooked up about Raj...?'

His hand went like python snake around my waist and he pulled me to his chest.

I took deep breath, of air, of Tarzan, his deo, his perfume. 'Then why didn't you come out of night club with thee others?' I asked, my voice thick like Heinz tomato ketchup.

'Someone had to settle the tab,' he replied, his voice smooth like Dabur honey.

My heart started singing and dancing like anything. Tarzan didn't have action scene at thee night club! *Oye balle- balle!*

His hand went to thee back of my head, pulling it back. 'No *dhoom dhoom* business with anyone before or after that either,' he answered thee questions I didn't ask, staring down into my eyes. 'Got back to the hotel with the others.'

Another doubt was waiting in line, *ji*, in my heart and he cleared that also.

'As for the Simran episode, she and Dumpy had a major showdown...I'm surprised you didn't hear them...Andeep was with Dumpy, I thought I'd comfort Simran... terrible idea in hindsight, I'll give you that –'

Thee sight of Simran making kissy face at him came back to my mind. 'You like to comfort young girls?' I asked in acid voice.

'Only if the young girl's you.' He bent down and joined lips with me.

Bas, I leaped up on tippy-toes, threw my arms around his neck and pounced on his lips. Thee way I attacked thee rest of him! Snatching his jacket away, pulling his buttons, almost tearing his shirt. *Hai*, I *toh* had become thee horndog. All I could think of was sex with Tarzan, all night long, on all thee furnitures. I knew it was because of thee hormones, but I'd lost all control.

He lost control also, and soon, we were on thee bed doing thee *kaand* (oho, understand by yourself, should I explain each and every word?)

I remembered something suddenly and reached for thee night lamp. Tried to switch it off, but his hand caught mine.

'I've put on weight –' I cried like small puppy under tractor wheels, covering my tummy with my hands.

'You're perfect,' He pushed my hands away. 'I missed you, baby. Remember the last time we did this,' he whispered, kissing my stomach, 'we didn't have our friend here.' He put one hand in his backside – means, jeans backside pocket, and took out thee condom which we'd received as return home gift from Bangkok restaurant.

My heart became twisted. I could never in my life forget thee last time. We'd made up one week after thee maid-bastard fight and were both mad for humpy-pumpy, jumpy-tumpy, bangy-bangy. That night there was no condom at home and anyways it was too late (not in thee night, in thee live action). We'd said bye-bye to protection. And I'd said hello to pregnancy.

Oho, I didn't want to keep it secret from Tarzan. I *toh* wanted to tell him thee day I found out. But life's like Indian monsoon, highly unpredictable. *Maa@#* we think something in life and something else happens. Making our whole life upside down.

My mind flashbacked to thee day I'd taken thee pregnancy test, that *susu* one.

'I want to tell you something,' I told Tarzan. He'd come back from work and we were chill-maaroing on thee sofa.

'I want to tell you something, too,' he said, putting his hand inside my popcorn bowl. 'You go first.'

'No, you go.' I thought I'd finish thee popcorns in my mouth till then.

'Okay,' he began, placing his legs on thee centre table, 'remember Pranav and Tina – my friends from uni?'

'Ya, ya,' I moved my head up and down.

I think I did SRK-type overacting, because he started shaking his head. 'You don't have a clue, do you?'

Hai, he *toh* knew me so well.

I gave him 'I'm-sorry' look.

He gave me 'It's-okay' look, stuffing popcorns into his mouth.

'Tell what happened to Pavan and Bina?'

'Pranav and Tina.'

'Ya, ya.' I was getting highly impatient to share my news.

'Yeah, I heard from them after ages...so, get this, these guys were happily unmarried...in a relationship for seven years, living in for five...it was all smooth sailing, when – bam – she discovers she's preggers...'

I sat up straight. Was it sign from above? We sharing thee same news at thee same time?

I was so excited, I almost didn't hear what Tarzan was saying. '...Jeez, they had no idea what hit them... they were in shock for days...'

'Then?' I asked in rough voice.

'What else, they felt compelled to get married...had sworn they never would...I mean, they were practically the founders of the Anti-Marriage Squad and the Childfree by Choice Club...' Tarzan gave bitter laugh.

My mouth fell to thee floor as thee words finally went in my ears.

He went on, '...said what choice did they have...felt it was the right thing to do under the circumstances... had to take the responsibility...now their life's gone for a toss, everything's gone to shit...trapped into it...all because of one small mistake...'

I stopped listening after that. My dreams mixed with dirt. My hopes were crushum-crushed. It was sign from above. Tarzan didn't want to get married or have children. I wanted to, but not at thee cost of my self respect. I didn't want him to feel pressurised. I didn't want him to feel trapped. I didn't want his life to 'go to shit wit' because of me.

15

The one with the cat and the bag and all that jazz

When I moved in with him, I'd thought we'd get married – not immediately, but in few months. I'd thought we'd have children – not immediately, but in a few years. I never thought he'd continue to have same anti attitude towards both thee things.

I didn't want him to marry me because he felt he'd no choice or because it was thee right thing to do or because he felt responsible. I wanted him to marry me because he felt love, nothing else but love.

'That's it, I guess. The long and short of it,' he finished both thee popcorn and his story. 'What's your news?'

Everything in my body was paining: my throat, my eyes, my heart. I don't know how I opened my mouth, how I forced myself to speak. 'Dingy called, she and Andeep are going to get engaged.' I said thee first thing that came to my head.

He kept thee popcorn bowl down between us. 'That's amazing! You must be so happy.'

'I am.' My voice was shaking. 'So happy.'

'Aww, look at you.' He misunderstood my tears for happiness and pulled me into tight hug. 'My baby.'

I put my head on his shoulder and cried for *my* baby.

My flashback ended then and there, but tears started running down my cheek.

Tarzan stopped kissing my stomach and sat up up on thee bed, saying, 'Hey, hey, hey.'

He wiped my tear away, his hands gentler than Johnson Baby Soap.

I adjusted my clothes, covered my stomach and sat up, too.

He put his arms around me. 'It's going to be all right, Mahi, we're going to be all right, baby,' he whispered, resting his chin on my head.

He was trying to calm me, but that made me cry even more. Because I knew inside my heart that we'd never be.

'Dance, Mahi, dance,' Dumpy said, holding both my hands up.

Sangeet function was on full flow. Sweety Aunty (Dingy's mother) was playing thee *dholki*, Auntyji (Andeep's mother) was hitting it loudly with steel spoon, Pammiji (my stepmother, Bhooto) was singing '*Rail gaddi*' song at thee top of her lungs. Luckily, her voice wasn't as bad as her health.

Uncleji (Andeep's father) had already broken one whiskey glass. He was moving both hands like he was operating handpump with Glass Number Two on his head. Niku, Gurdeep, her husband and kids, Dingy, Andeep, had formed train and were running around thee Riverside Verandah like cracks.

But thee last thing I wanted to do was join in. I'd walked out of Niku's room, my heart pieces-pieces. Tarzan had tried to stop me, kept asking me what was wrong, kept trying to make me to talk to him, but I what could I say?

I wanted to go to one corner and cry, but I remembered my promise to Dingy. Thee weekend was about her. My life, my tensions, my problems could wait.

I made my heart hard and became compartment in thee train. Suddenly, I felt two warm hands around my waist. Tarzan!

I *toh* didn't dare to look behind or snatch them away. I turned round, I broke thee chain and went to thee bar. Tarzan compartment also left thee train and followed me.

Thee bar had been set up next to thee coconut tree. Alcohol was flowing. And most of it was going inside thee family bartender – Dumpy's – stomach. That was okay, he'd capacity of tanker. But he was forcing Simran and Raj to drink.

Simran *toh* could hold her drink. But Raj could not. He – means, his bladder – had capacity of small baby. I was sure that Raj was one sip away from doing *susu* in public.

Dumpy mixed vodka, whiskey, rum in one empty Absolut bottle and poured one shot down Raj's throat. Then came Simran's turn. Then Tarzan's. Then he turned to me.

I gave him my strict headmaster look. 'I'm off drinks-shinks.'

'What off-shoff?' he ignored my warning with wave of his hand, 'Here, come, open your mouth. Take one sip and see, you'll forget everything –'

'I said no, Dumpy. No means no,' I said in '*kutte-*don't-take-*panga*' tone.

'What, *yaar*, Mahi,' he protested, 'what's this new *natak*?'

'I'm not doing drama, Dumpy.'

'It's Dingy's wedding, Dingy's,' he repeated like I didn't know. 'How can you not be *talli*? It's your duty.'

Arre, where it was written that it was duty to be drunk at your BFF's wedding?

'Drink, drink, drink, drink, drink,' Raj started chanting.

'Shut up, Raj! You want to do *susu* in public, you do. I've better things to do.'

Tarzan looked as if I'd cracked funny joke. But he didn't force me. Or try to stop me when I walked away from thee bar.

'What happened to her, *yaar*?' I heard Dumpy ask aloud. 'She used to beat all of us in drinking competitions.'

I went and sat next to Bhooto. It was better to become deaf than give explanation to everyone.

Dumpy and gang came to thee verandah few minutes later. Big shot bottle was still in his hand and he started serving it like holy water at temples to everyone, straight into their mouths.

After finishing thee Auntyjis, he reached me.

'Oye, Dingy,' he yelled, 'see what your best friend's doing. Not drinking at your wedding.'

Dingy and Andeep did 'Drink, drink' action with their hands without leaving thee train.

I shook my head and got up. I was going to walk away, but Dumpy blocked my way.

'That's it, enough of acting,' he said, catching one hand. 'I'll see how she doesn't –'

Raj came forward and caught my other hand.

'Leave me, Dumpy!' I shouted, turning my face this way and that.

My stomach started churning in fear. I didn't know what to do, how to stop them. What could I say? 'Don't do it, I'm pregnant?'

Dumpy lifted thee bottle and was about to pour thee shot in my mouth, when Simran cried out, *'Don't do it, she's pregnant!'*

It was like someone had pressed on thee pause button on thee remote control. Thee chatting, thee music, thee dancing, thee eating, thee train, everything stopped. Uncleji Auntyji quickly covered thee ears of Gurdeep's children with their hands. As if by listening to my story, their grandchildren would become corrupted.

For one minute, I *toh* went blank. Like one stupid, my first thought was, 'Simran had looked inside my medicine pouch'.

I stood like statue, not having thee guts to look at Tarzan.

Before I could have second thought, everyone started talking at thee same time.

'It's not mine! She forced me to act like her boyfriend. I didn't want to, but she said she'd give me assistant job if I cooperated. But I didn't touch her, God promise.' That was Raj. He'd been flying high, looking like *Udta Punjab*, he came down to earth like *this*.

'Told you, *na*, Mr. America couldn't be trusted. Now see what he's done.' That was Dumpy. He looked like he'd achieved major victory in life.

'How could you, Lavith? Had I known, I'd have never ever taken your help.' That was Niku. He looked like he wanted to press Tarzan's neck with his hands.

'First your father, now you. Thee men in your family have no self-control or what? Why can't you keep your snake in your pant?' That was Bhooto. She looked like she wanted to join Niku in murdering Tarzan.

'Thanks, Mahi, thanks for making me Number-Two again.' That was Dingy. She burst out crying and ran away from thee spot.

'Trying to kiss Lavith wasn't enough for you, Simran? You had to tell this also to everyone and ruin Dingy's wedding? You're happy now?' That was me.

Everyone gasped, Dumpy thee loudest. I didn't want to hurt Dumpy, but thee words were out of my mouth before I could stop myself.

I was trying badly to make my BFF's dream come true, but Simran had made Dingy's nightmare come true. Made someone else – okay, okay, me – thee centre of attraction at her wedding.

I didn't care who was listening, who was thinking what. I didn't care about thee world or society. Where were they when Niku or Tarzan or I was going through bad time in life? They were happily gossiping and enjoying. Only my family, my best friends were there for us. They were thee only ones I cared about.

I turned to follow Dingy. That's when I saw Tarzan. Thee look on his face! He looked as if he'd received *sazaa-e-maut* (oho, hanging death punishment) from thee court of life.

I'm not scared of anyone's Dad in life. No, *ji*, not. But that look! That was thee look I never ever wanted to see on his face. That's why I'd walked out of his flat when he was out of the country. That's why I never ever wanted to discuss thee topic with him.

Bas, I couldn't take it anymore. Tears started running down my face and I walked away from him as fast as I could.

We were sitting alone – Niku, Bhooto and me and having square table conversation.

I'd gone straight to Dingy's room, knocked and asked sorry thousand times. But she didn't open thee door or her mouth.

That's how Niku and Bhooto found me. Banging like anything.

'I want to kill that @#$%,' Niku growled, punching his fist into his hand.

I closed my eyes as if he'd attacked me. My little Niku giving abuse. Niku was so sweet, so soft, so gentle. I'd seen him like this only once before in life. When he didn't have money to start his own business.

'I'll call up Neeru right now, let her also know what flowers her son has been growing behind her backside,' Bhooto muttered.

As if Tarzan was second-standard boy who had rung our doorbell and run away.

'Mummyji, please.'

'What please? Had I known was *awara aiyash badmash*, I'd have never sent you to Delhi.'

Tarzan wasn't loose-charactered rascal, I knew that inside my heart. How I could think he'd done bad-bad things like lap dancing with strippers or kissing with Simran? My brain had gone to eat grass.

'He's not, Mummyji.' I protested. 'Please stop blaming him. Two people make baby.'

'Yes, yes, Lavith's father and Lavith,' she spat thee words. 'They are experts at making babies.'

'It's no one's fault,' I said calmly, 'these things happen.'

Bhooto was in no mood to be calm. 'These things happen only to that family. I think so it's their family business. Have fun with innocent girls and leave them when they get pregnant.'

'That's not true Mummyji.'

'Then tell truth,' Niku said.

Suddenly, his words from earlier in thee evening came back to me.

'Niku, one minute…you told Lavith "Had I known, I'd have never taken your help"…when did you take help?'

Thee answer came to me by itself.

'You took money from Lavith? For your ASS? For your business?' I gasped.

Niku turned redder than Dingy's wedding *lehenga*.

'Niku! When? I never knew – you didn't even tell. How could you keep such big secret from me?'

'Same way you kept such big thing secret from me,' he replied. 'Don't worry, it was before you broke up with him and came back to Ludhiana. I'm not that cheap also.'

We gave each other dirty looks.

'Whatever happened, happened,' Bhooto said sadly. 'Family means trust. Now we've to stop keeping secrets from each other. Okay?'

Suddenly, I felt sad. Oho, not because I fought with Niku, because if Bhooto said thee most sensible thing in thee room, then there was something very wrong in life.

We used to say such big-big things. That we were like own brother and sister, that we were *more* than own brother sister. Then why hadn't I trusted him? Why hadn't he trusted me?

'I didn't want you to get worried.'

'I didn't want you to get worried.'

Niku and I gave answer at thee same time.

He jumped to his feet and came over to give me tight hug.

'Sorry, sorry, sorry, Mahi.'

'Give me sorry, Niku. No more secrets, no more fighting, let's agree.'

'I agree,' Bhooto replied on his behalf. 'Hope that Lavith also agrees for marriage.'

I turned to her and said in firm voice. 'Mummyji, there will be no marriage. He never wanted to get married –'

'That was before. Things are different now, *puttar*.'

'No, Mummyji, if he's not interested, I'm not interested. I can take care of myself.'

'But –'

'She's right, Mummyji,' Niku took my side. 'Why should she live with someone who doesn't want to live with her?'

'But how will you manage?' Bhooto cried. 'It's not easy being single mother.'

'Many mothers have done it,' Niku said like he was authority on single mothers.

'Name one,' Bhooto challenged.

'Preity Zinta –'

WWW? Preity Zinta had baby? So soon after marriage? *Arre*, what was thee hurry burry?

'In *Kya Kehna*. In thee beginning, things were tough, later everything became all right.' Niku finished.

'That was movie, real life is different, you cannot even imagine how tough life will become. Please don't misunderstand me, *puttar*, I'm not thinking of thee society, I'm thinking about you. Please please –'

I got up to signal that it was thee end of discussion.

'I'm not going to change my mind, Mummyji.'

'Ya,' she said, wiping her eyes with her dupatta, 'why will you listen to me, I'm only stepmother. If your real mother was here…'

I was seeing repeat telecast of *Bechari Bhooto* serial. She'd done thee same drama, given thee same dialogues, when I'd announced my living-in.

I flashbacked into that day in Delhi.

16

The one with multiple torture scenes

We were sitting in thee drawing room of our house, having square table meeting. I'd called my cabinet – oho, all thee important people in my life, (except Tarzan because I'd already informed him about my decision).

I was standing. Bhooto, Niku, Dumpy, Dingy, Sukhna were sitting.

'Thank you for coming. Mummyji, please, can you leave that pakora…'

Bhooto dropped thee pakora back in thee plate and picked up samosa from another.

'…and thee samosa…'

Bhooto left thee samosa like she was making ultimate sacrifice. She leaned back on thee sofa, but her eyes never left thee food.

'Please give me hundred percent of your attention.'

Concerned look came on Niku's face. 'You're okay, *na*, Mahi. Not in trouble – ?'

'Oye, trouble is mad or what to take *panga* with her,' Dumpy waved his worry away, stuffing his mouth with masala peanuts.

'Or ill,' Niku completed.

'Ill?' Dumpy brayed like donkey. 'Look at her, strong like bull.'

'Then why have you called all of us like this, suddenly, in thee middle of Sunday afternoon?' Dingy asked.

'Ya, that's what I'm telling,' Niku agreed.

'She hates being disturbed on her holiday,' Dingy added.

'Stopped me from eating and not telling also.'

I peesoed my teeth. If they would let me talk only, no.

I put my hands on my ears and shouted 'AAAAAAAAAA!'

Everyone put their tongues inside their mouths.

'Nothing's wrong. I'm not in trouble, thank you, Niku, for your concern. I'm healthy, thank you Dumpy, for thee vote of confidence. I wanted to share something with you all.'

'Lavith's proposed!' Dingy screamed, jumping up.

'You're getting married?' Dumpy asked.

'Yes and no.'

Everyone went blink-blink.

'Lavith had proposed. In Chennai. When she'd gone to save him,' Niku spoke to himself.

'That's old story,' Dingy interrupted. 'Did he propose to you now, Mahi? Did he ask his parents to talk to Pammi Aunty and set thee date?'

Uff!

These people were interrupting me like that news channel anchor.

I held up my hand. 'Please, can thee questions come after my breaking news?'

'Lavith's proposed. But not for marriage. For living in relationship. And I've said yes.'

There was graveyard-type silence in thee room.

Then Bhooto started slapping her forehead.

'It's all my fault. My brain was dead. I shouldn't have let you go to Delhi alone to meet him so many times. Like one donkey I thought if you stayed in my sister's house, you'd be safe, but I was wrong. *Hai, hai*, what black magic that *kameena* boy's done on my flower-like child –'

'Mummyji, please, control.'

'Why, Mahi, why?' Dingy cried.

'Why he's asked me or why I've said yes?'

'Both,' Dumpy replied.

'He's asked me because it's practical. I can't keep going to Delhi, he can't keep coming to Ludhiana –'

After I'd saved Tarzan from thee Chennai floods, he'd gone back to New York. He'd resigned from his job, sold his flat and furniture and moved to Delhi.

'*Arre*, what's more practical than marriage,' Bhooto cut in. 'Best solution to your travel problem, best solution to all thee problems in life,' Bhooto insisted.

Uff!

Typical Indian attitude. Boy can't lift ding-dong? Get him married. Girl working and becoming "too independent"? Get her married.

'I know you love him – we all love him, but –' Niku began, looking tensed means tensed.

'But can you trust him?' Dumpy asked.

'Yes, I can.' I was more confident about thee answer than any participant on KBC (not *Kaun Banega Chutiya*, thee real show).

'You don't know these American fellows –' Dumpy insisted.

'How many American fellows do you know, Dumpy?' I challenged him.

He was going to open his mouth, but I added, 'Don't count thee heroes of thee movies you watch.' He shut his mouth.

'But what if he leaves you after few months?' Bhooto asked, her eyes wider than her waist.

'He's not like that, Mummyji. And if he has to break up, he can do that after marriage also.'

Bhooto started slapping her chest.

'I thought you liked him, Mummyji.'

'That was before he proposed, when I thought he was normal.'

'He's normal, Mummyji. He did it because he loves me.'

'If he loves you, Mahi, why can't he get married to you?' Dingy insisted.

I'd also asked myself thee same question. But I'd explained to myself that Tarzan was different. His thinking was different, more Western. He'd lived in America for ten years, in his adult years. And his childhood years in India, *toh* don't ask. They were really *tatti*. So he was more *Phoren* Gentleman than *Desi* Boy.

'See, our courts allow trial period before divorce, no? Why can't we have trial period before marriage?' I argued. 'I'm not saying we'll never get married. But not right now. Right now, we want to find out more about each other, our likes, dislikes –'

'Mahi, *puttar*,' Mummyji cried: 'I understand that you both want to enjoy life. But if you get married, we all can enjoy together. Please don't misunderstand me, I'm not saying all this because I'm worried "What will people say". I'm saying all this because I'm worried about you…'

I sat down on thee table and took her hands. 'Mummyji, do you trust me?'

She nodded.

'Then, please, stop crying, stop worrying. Nothing will happen to me. You heard Dumpy, I'm strong as bull.'

She wiped her eyes. 'Ya, ya, why will you listen to me, I'm not your real mother...'

'If you've made up your mind, what can we say?' Niku muttered.

'You can say congrats,' I said softly.

He bent forward, put his arms around me and gave me tight hug. Dingy joined in. Dumpy kept distance and kept shaking his head. Meeting got over. So did my flashback.

But Bhooto did not. Even in thee present, she kept going sob-sob, sniff-sniff, *hai-hai*.

I smiled.

Hain?

What was happening to me? Instead of getting irritated, I was smiling at Bhooto's overacting! *Hai*, I *toh* was losing my mental balance.

'If you really lov –' I corrected myself, 'if you really care about me, Mummyji, promise me that you'll not talk about marriage to Lavith or to Neeru Aunty.'

I patted her hand for few more minutes. Then I told them bye and stepped out of thee room.

And immediately got heart attack.

Tarzan was standing there. 'We need to talk.'

'No, we don't.' I tried to walk away. But he blocked my way.

'Don't push it, Mahi,' he said in warning tone. 'We're going to do this whether you like it or not. Now, what's it going to be? Are you going to come with me to the gym voluntarily or do I have to –'

He made sudden move as if he was going to lift me up and put me on his shoulder like gunny bag.

I gulped. He looked like forest animal, capable of doing anything. 'No need to be rude,' I said, tossing my head.

'*This* close,' he threatened, making close sign with his thumb and index finger to show his patience tank was empty.

'Anyways, I wanted to check out thee gym.' I said quickly, not taking chance.

I started walking with him, practising my speech inside my head. His body was hot stove. I could feel thee anger waves coming from it.

Thee second we entered thee gym, he switched on all thee lights. It was so bright, I'd to close my eyes. Immediately, I was reminded of torture scene from one Hollywood movie I'd seen.

He went and sat down on workout bench like he wanted to press me. 'Explain.'

I went and stood near thee heavyweights to show him I wasn't less.

I opened my mouth to speak, but my head was empty. I'd forgotten thee *kambakth* speech I'd prepared.

'It's not yours,' I said thee first thing that came inside my head.

Thee vein in his forehead jumped dangerously. 'I'll give you another chance, Mahi. Try again.'

Arre, it was PT class or what?

He started getting up from thee bench.

'Okay, okay, I didn't tell you because it's not your problem –'

'It's not?'

'No. It's my problem – means, it's no problem…'

Uff!

That was thee problem, I didn't know what I was talking.

I took yoga breath. 'I didn't want you to feel pressurised. I didn't want your life to go for toss. I –'

'I see,' He interrupted, his voice like acid. 'So you were being cruel to be kind.'

'I didn't want to force you to take responsibility you didn't want,' I continued.

'And you know what I want?'

'Yes, you want to live carefree, happy life...'

'I do,' he agreed. 'With you.'

Tears started to come out, but with great difficulty I swallowed them.

'You aren't ready to settle down, Lavith.'

'Ready or not, this baby's my responsibility.'

My heart squeezed like empty Colgate toothpaste tube. Oho, I never expected him to say, 'But I'm ready!', but still, thee truth was painful to hear.

'Don't worry, Lavith, I'm freeing you from it.'

His mouth twisted in bitter smile. 'Thank you for deciding everything for me, Mahi.'

'You'll thank me later –'

'I'm thanking you right now.'

'Oho, why you're not understanding.' I cried, throwing my hands up. 'This is not some funny joke –'

'Well, you did a fine job of making a mockery out of our relationship.'

'I didn't make mock – hello, one minute – what relationship are you talking about? You've got Aamir Khan's problem in *Ghajni* or what? Forgot thee bitter fights we used to have? Please, Lavith, you want something else in life, I want something else –'

He looked at me like I was doing heavy torture to him. 'What do you want, Mahi?'

My shoe, I'd tell him. My foot, I'd beg him.

'Was there anything missing in our relationship?' he growled.

Love. Marriage. Children.

'Commitment? Loyalty? Trust?' he went on. 'Didn't we have that and more? I thought – I really thought we understood each other, Mahi. I thought we wanted the same things –'

I stared at him not able to believe. He was mad or what? He thought I wanted to be in living-in relationship till I was ninety-year old oldie?

'We decided to get into it together.'

That was *toh* thee limit only.

'No!' I shouted. 'I didn't decide. You decided. You asked, "Why don't you move in?" I said "Okay, fine".'

He looked like I'd give him tight slap. 'Wait, you were not fine with it?'

My expression was clear. How I could be fine with it? As if it was some normal thing like cough-cold. And everyone in India had it at some point or thee other in life.

'Wow, this is news to me,' he said slowly. 'If you did have any reservations, why didn't you say something –'

'Because I didn't want to break up with you!'

Dark look came on his face. 'So you're saying I arm-twisted you, I emotionally blackmailed you into moving in with me?'

Arre, why was he putting his things into my mouth?

'No, Lavith,' I said patiently. 'I'm saying you gave suggestion, I tried to see it from your point of view, I thought about it and –'

He walked up to me and looked down into my eyes, his eyes like big balls (oho, of fire). 'But did you extend me the same courtesy? You felt it wasn't working out, you decided to end things,' he growled. 'You didn't even give me – us – a chance. You just upped and left, no discussion, nothing.'

'There was,' I said in choked voice, 'there is nothing to discuss.'

'Actually, I'm with you on this one,' he agreed. 'If my memory serves me right, we're almost three months along.'

We?

Hain?

When did I make him pregnant?

'We're getting married right away, Mahi.'

My heart had breakdown. That's what I was afraid of. Marriage proposal out of duty, responsibility, force. Marriage proposal without love. He'd said 'I love you' when I'd saved him in Chennai. But not once after that. No, *ji*, not. I think so he was scared that if he said thee three words, I'd say thee three words ('Let's get married').

'No, we're not, Lavith.'

'Don't be stupid –'

'I'm not interested in getting married to you –'

His hands were on my shoulders and he didn't realize he was shaking me. 'Do you know what it's like to be *illegitimate*?' He said thee word like it was abuse. 'To carry the weight of that word around? To live your life knowing that you're not wanted by the person who brought you into the world?'

I didn't know, but I knew what it was like to be in relationship without love.

'Have you even thought the whole thing through? You think living with the "unwed mother" tag's going to be a breeze in a small town like Ludhiana?'

What did he think of me? That I was so *jhalli*, so stupid that I didn't know that much?

'First of all,' I began. 'Ludhiana's not small town. It's city. Second of all, I've thought of everything. After one month, I'm moving to Mumbai, big city, where no one knows me.'

'And when people ask you about the father of the baby?'

'I'll say he's dea –' I saw his expression and changed my answer quickly. 'Divorced.'

I pushed his hands from my shoulders and took one step back. From him, from thee discussion.

'I know how you feel, Lavith, but –'

He pushed his hand inside his hair. He always did like that when he was in tension. 'You can't possibly know how I feel.'

'I'm sorry, but I cannot marry you. Not for thee wrong reason.'

'Having a baby together isn't reason enough?'

No, you duffer, I wanted to shout. It's not enough, I want more. But how could I? Oho, I wasn't being proudy or giving him attitude, I was giving myself respect. If he didn't understand this much by himself, what was thee point? He'd said we understood each other. I'd understood him, but my shoe only he'd understood me. He *toh* didn't know thee M of Mahi.

I decided to give him one last chance. 'But you always said you wanted to see thee world, eat at every restaurant with three stars –'

'Three Michelin stars,' he corrected.

'...have exciting adventures, new experiences. But marriage, children, staying in one place, sticking to same routine? Is that thee life you want for yourself?'

'It's not the life I'd imagined for sure, I'll give you that,' he confessed. 'But that's life, Mahi, it constantly surprises you and –'

Bas, I didn't want to listen to one more word. I'd got what I wanted, thee answer I was looking for. Finally, I was cent-percent sure that I was taking thee right decision.

'You're wrong, Lavith.' My heart was broken glass, my voice was steel. 'You should get the life you always imagined. Anyways, let's not talk about this anymore. My decision is final. I'm not interested in you or marriage. So, please, leave me alone. Okay ta-ta bye-bye.'

I walked out of thee gym with straight shoulder, without backward look.

17

In which the air is cleared and bridges (at least, some of them) are mended

'You've still not eaten?' Bhooto slapped her forehead, looking at my untouched food tray. '*Rabba*, what's wrong with this girl. Close thee laptop now, look at thee time. If not for yourself, eat for –' She didn't finish thee sentence. She picked up thee edge of her dupatta and started wiping her eyes.

It was few days after thee wedding. We were back in Ludhiana. I'd already announced my decision – thee Mumbai one – to her and Niku. They had taken thee news so badly, cried so much that I was worried thee whole Ahluwalia *tabbar* (oho, family) would move to Mumbai.

But how I could be so selfish? Bhooto's kitty parties, her BBFs (oho, Bank Balance Friends), Niku's business, his close friends, their whole life was in Ludhiana. So I'd used *Brahmastra* (oho, deadly heavenly weapon). I'd put both their hands on my head and given them my swear. They would stay back or else they would see-see my dead face.

They had already seen my half-dead face in *Hawa-Hawai* island. I'd not even smiled even when Muesli had gifted me five free hotel tee shirts. Also, he'd spoilt everything by adding, 'Please give us five-star rating on Tlip Advisol, Madame'. As if I'd take bribe-shibe to say good-good things about Lembla Resort on Trip Advisor.

Anyways, leave. My heart was in too much pain. I'd hidden my inside feelings from thee world, but my family knew thee inside truth.

Tarzan had left thee resort soon after our gym discussion. I got to know only next day, on thee day of wedding. I felt really upsetted and hurted by his behaviour. Oho, not because he didn't have thee courtesy to tell me goodbye, because he didn't have thee courtesy to stay back and wish Andeep and Dingy happy married life.

Then, I thought, good only he left. I could work in peace. And I did. I acted like complete professional. Made sure thee execution was as perfect as my idea. That was my surprise gift for Dingy.

So, in our Punjoo tradition, thee bride enters thee *mandap* area walking below *Phoolon ki Chaadar* (oho, canopy of flowers) carried by her brothers, cousins, friends. But I wanted nothing less than grand hero's entry for my BFF. That's why I'd organized special topless tuk-tuk.

Thee scene when Dingy entered thee wedding area, standing on it, wearing deep red *lehenga choli* and matching golden Aviators – *oye hoye*, don't ask – it was *ghaint* (oho, cool-shool, awesome-*shaw*some). Everyone's mouths fell down.

Amanjeet (Andeep's brother-in-law) *toh* got so excited, he brought out pistol from his pocket and was going to fire shots in thee air.

Uff!

Just because you have gun licence doesn't mean you've license to act like donkey. Typical mentality. Doing local nonsense at international level.

Luckily, Dumpy jumped on up and pulled him down before he could pull thee trigger. Or Andeep would have been honeymooning with male prisoners in Thailand jail.

Honeymoon. Thee word brought tears to my eyes. Oho, not because I would never have one with Lavith, but because I'd fulfilled my promise to Dingy. I'd made sure she did bang-bang in Bangkok.

Dingy. Thee word made me even sadder. Oho, not because she was moving to Delhi after her marriage, but because she was still not talking to me. I'd broken my promise to Dingy. I'd made her look like Number-Two (not shit, secondary topic) at her own wedding.

I was hundred-percent sure that even in Ludhiana thee Number-One topic of discussion was Mother Mahi. But if Bhooto or Niku had heard something, if anyone had called them to get gossip, they didn't tell me. I *toh* was least interested to ask. Dogs bark, elephants quietly walk away.

TING TONG! TING TONG!

Thee doorbell rang broke my thoughts.

'Sukhna's gone to thee market. I'll go and see,' Bhooto said, rushing out.

I switched off my laptop, walked to thee side table and picked up my food tray. My room door opened:

THAANNNNN!

I dropped thee food tray, my mouth open in surprise.

Dingy was standing there! Bride Dingy! In bright pink suit and red bangles almost till her underarms.

'Mahi!' She ran in and threw herself on me.

'Dingy! What are you doing here? I thought you were in Bangkok.'

'I couldn't stay away from you, Mahi!'

Hai, she had cut Andeep – means, cut her honeymoon with Andeep, because she was missing me.

'Mahi-ve, lakh-lakh sorry. I behaved so badly, didn't talk to you, didn't say thank you. You did so much for me, you made me thee happiest person in thee whole world. And what did I do? I ignored you in your bad time. I'm so sorr –' she burst out crying.

'I'm sorry, Dingy,' I burst out, my eyes becoming taps. 'I didn't want people to talk about me, I wanted you and your wedding to be thee talk of thee town –'

'And we are, Mahi, we are,' she said, wiping her nose. 'Andeep gave his swear to his family, dare they said anything about what happened to anyone back in India. No one knows about your news, but everyone knows about Dingy's tuk-tuk entry.'

For thee first time since my return, I smiled.

So what if Mahi's personal life was shit and shocking?

Her professional life was hit and rocking.

We wiped each other's tears and talked – okay, okay, gossiped thee whole afternoon. I didn't tell her about my Mumbai decision – I thought why to spoil her mood again? But she told me everything. What all she'd done in Bangkok (in detail), about her new family (they were not so bad also), about Dumpy and Simran (they had broken up). About Tarzan.

He'd gone to Chennai for one week. Oho, he had house there. He'd been wanting to sell it, but something or thee other kept happening and it kept getting postponed. First, he was busy drowning in thee floods, then he was busy shifting to India, then he was busy working like mad dog, then he was busy fighting with me, then he was busy starting his new business.

Anyways, after Dingy left, I felt lightum-light. If my loved ones were okay, everything in life was okay.

I switched on thee TV to do some time-pass. Thee news channel was on and as usual, thee anchor was yelling. I was going to change thee channel, when my hand got stuckum-stuck to thee remote.

'Cyclone Vardah devastates Chennai...life comes to a standstill...heavy rainfall...widespread destruction...'

Scary scenes filled thee TV screen. Fallen trees, electricity poles, lamp-posts. Upside-down cars, autos, shipping containers. Missing roofs, broken windows, waterlogged roads.

I stood like statue, not able to believe my ears or eyes.

Someone had pressed rewind button in my life.

Tarzan had gone to Chennai to die again.

Last year, he'd had lucky escape. What would happen this year?

It was thee day after thee cyclone. I was in Chennai, in local taxi. I'd contacted Andeep thee minute I'd heard thee news. Thanks to God Chennai Airport had reopened. *Bas*, I'd rushed to Delhi and taken thee first flight.

Bhooto had begged and cried, asked me not to do dangerous things in my state, but I'm like Bhai (not Niku, Salman). Once I make commitment, I don't even listen to myself.

'I don't know how to thank you, Rakesh,' I said in sincere voice. 'I'm so grateful to you.'

Rakesh was Andeep's bua's daughter's – oho, he was Andeep's reporter friend from Delhi. He'd come with me to Chennai to save Tarzan last year, too.

'Not grateful enough apparently,' he muttered.

'What?'

'The name's Dinesh. D-I-N-E-S-H, Dinesh.'

That was thee problem with him. He was good fellow, but even during emergency situation, he was bothered about silly things like name.

'Okay, okay,' I said in soothing voice. 'Please, ask thee driver how long it will take us to reach Kott...Kottu...'

We'd been stuck in traffic jam for more than one hour.

Rakesh leaned forward in his seat. 'Pah, how long will it take us to reach Kotturpuram, pah?'

Arre, why was he making thee taxi-driver his Daddy?

'Local parlance for "friend or *yaar*",' he explained, seeing my confused look.

We didn't speak anything else during thee journey. I was in too much tension. I'd tried to call Tarzan thousand and one times, but *kambakht* mobile networks were down. I'd called Neeru Aunty and Dhiren Uncle, too. They were in bad shape. I'd promised them that I'd be back with good news (oho, not THAT good news, good news about their son) soon.

Thee taxi stopped suddenly, cutting my thoughts.

'What happ – ?'

I gasped as I saw in front. There was no road. Only fallen trees from here to there. It was as if we were standing in forest.

'Could you try another route, please?' Rakesh asked thee driver. 'The lady here has to rescue her –'

'Family friend,' I supplied thee missing information.

'Family friend, really?' Rakesh was fully fed up. I'd given him same bull-and-cock story last year. 'You're still going with that?'

I gave him wooden look. *Arre*, I didn't want to tell my personal life to every Tom, Dick, Harpeet.

'Saar, do something. There must be another way,' Rakesh please-pleased.

'Chance-ey *illa*,' thee taxi driver refused.

I paid and we got down.

'*F@#$! F@#$! F@#$!*' Rakesh cursed.

We started walking and kept going for one hour – oho, it felt like one hour – in some forest, asking people for direction.

'That, that's his street!' I shouted as we reached familiar place.

Thee street, like all thee streets we'd crossed, was filled with bent trees, fallen trees and people trying to clear fallen trees.

Suddenly, I stopped. My heart started beating badly. In the middle of thee street was tall, broad man in bright pink tee shirt. I'd given Tarzan that tee as our first month anniversary gift! I couldn't see thee man's face, but I knew in my heart it was him.

My hopes climbing up, I started walking fast-fast towards him. I'd almost reached him when huge branch fell from bent tree, crushing him.

I screamed!

I don't know what happened next. I think so I died and went up to heaven.

Because when I opened my eyes, my head was in Tarzan's lap.

'Mahi, Mahi.' I felt his hand on my cheek, water drops on my eyes.

Hai, there was so much pain in his voice.

'Lavith?' I blinked, looking up.

There was small crowd around us.

'Mahi? Oh thank god, you're okay, Mahi!' He bent down to hug me. 'Please, she needs some air,'

Thee crowd started walking away.

I looked at him, feeling relieved. Tarzan wasn't dead! Tarzan wasn't crushed like sugarcane stem! He was fine!

'For a moment, I thought –' he shivered, unable to finish thee sentence.

'That I was off?' I closed my eyes and stuck my tongue out, giving dead expression. 'I thought you were off too. I saw that tree fall on – oh, god,' I gasped, struggling to sit up. 'What happened to that poor fellow?'

'He's going to be fine, the volunteers are tending to him. But you, don't ever do that again.'

'Faint or come on rescue mission to save you?' I smiled weakly at him.

'Both.'

'Then don't keep coming to Chennai to die.'

'I promise,' he said, relief shining in his eyes. He reached for my hands. 'I love you, Mahi.'

I pulled my hands away. 'You only say that when I save your life, Lavith.'

'So not true.'

'Name one other time you told me that?' I challenged.

'God, I'm an idiot,' he groaned. 'But I was so afraid –'

I stared at him. Tarzan and afraid?

'That I'd mess things up, that you'd leave me. And you did. You abandoned me. Just like my –'

Hai, he was comparing me to his father.

'With him, I knew where things stood, but you leaving – it was just – I just went to pieces,' he swallowed, shaking his head. 'When I came back to that empty apartment, I'd never felt so empty, so alone.'

Tears started shining in my eyes.

'I knew I'd screwed up, I knew that. All I wanted was another chance. And when I discovered that we were pregnant –'

I *toh* didn't know why he kept saying he was also pregnant, but, by god, it sounded cute.

'You were shockum-shocked.'

Tarzan nodded. 'I was taken aback, yes, but I thought I finally had a chance to make amends, to make it up to you and to him or her.' He put his big hands out and put them gently on my small tummy.

Oh, I *toh* felt my heart go diggy-diggy.

'But all those things you said about your friends Prem and Romila?'

'Pranav and Tina,' he corrected.

Uff!

I *toh* didn't know why everyone was so bothered about names.

Anyways, I continued, 'I thought you didn't want me and baby. I didn't want to us to spoil your life, come between you and your dreams. You only said it wasn't thee life you'd imagined for yourself.'

'I'd never imagined I'd find love, Mahi. I'd never imagined I could be so happy. I'd never imagined someone as sorted as you could love someone as messed up like me. I –' His voice broke, repairing my broken heart. I'd put on weight, but suddenly I felt light as idli.

'You're not that bad also,' I said jokily.

'I am,' he insisted. 'But, boy, am I glad you see it that way.'

'I love you, Lavith.'

'I love you, Mahi, so, so much. Promise you'll never leave me again?'

'I promise,' I whispered, joining my hands in his, my life with his.

Someone cleared throat very loudly or God only knows how long we'd have sat hugging-shugging in thee middle of thee road.

We looked up. It was Rakesh. No…Mukesh? Brijesh? Oho, same difference.

'Set a date, will ya?' he said in disgusted voice.

'Can't wait,' Lavith said happily.

'Can't wait,' I repeated like happy *tota* (not hot girl, parrot).

About the Author

Vibha Batra writes for children, tweens, young adults, adults, and senior citizens. She can be found in quaint cafes in Chennai, hunched over her laptop, writing away like a woman possessed or on FB: facebook/vibhy.batra or Instagram: @vibhybatra.